UNCONVENTIONAL

REBECCA ROYCE

Printed in the United States of America

First Printing, 2018

ISBN 978-1-947672-41-3

Cover Artist: Crimson Phoenix Creations

www.rebeccaroyce.com

 Created with Vellum

DEAR READER

Dear Reader,

Thank you so much for picking up this book. Giovanna's journey has turned into such a favorite story to write! If you are unfamiliar with the format, this is a serial. That means this story is not complete. It comes to an appropriate end to this part of the story. But it isn't a happily ever after yet. There will be three parts to this book. While most serials are short (just about 10,000 words and 1-2 chapters) this one is a full length novel. All three of them will be novel length. I hope you love Giovanna, Maven, Chance and Banyan.

Best,

Rebecca Royce

www.rebeccaroyce.com

NOTE

Please Note:

I have gone out of my way to search for Fraternity and Sorority names not currently in use in real life. But if I have stumbled upon a real one, please note that I am writing about fictionalized places. In no way should the people or circumstances described in the fraternities be thought of as real places or representing real places. They are works of fiction and in no way meant to infringe on the copyright, reputation, or intellectual property of real life fraternal organizations.

Thanks!

Rebecca Royce

PART ONE
A VACATION FROM MYSELF

ONE

"Hey there, library."

The voice. The sound of it calling to me across the street on that cold, chilly morning when I walked alone down Chow Street toward my empty dorm reaches me, not from any distance away, but through time itself. It seems odd to hear it now. Lying on my bed, I close my eyes. The baby will be here soon. I've gone into labor, but no one knows. I haven't let anyone in on the news yet.

The contractions are five minutes apart. Soon, I'll get up and the trip to the hospital will begin. But this quiet moment is just for me.

I'm not ready yet for the fuss, as loving as the intent to deliver attention will be.

I just want, for one moment, to breathe and remember. To think of how I got here to this moment: twenty-five years old, ready to bring life into the world for the first time.

Really, everything I am and everything I will be can be traced to that moment five years earlier when the voice called out to me, 'hey there, library.' Five days before Christmas. When I was all alone in the world.

I CLUTCHED my black pea coat tightly around me to block out the wind. Head down, I watched my boots move as they made imprints in the snow with every step I took. I was alone at *Denberg College* for the entire holiday season, and I was getting a little bit tired of it. My parents were across the world in North Sentinel Island, India, seeing if they could get the Sentinelese to let them come onto the island. It was easier said than done, but my parents, the cultural anthropologists who both taught full time at Harvard, had managed this sort of feat before.

This left me, their daughter, who worked really hard but whose struggles with dyslexia left her less-than incredible in the academic department, alone on my college campus for the entire winter holiday this year.

I'd get to see them during the summer. Assuming the Sentinelese didn't shoot poison darts at them and kill them. They'd been known to do that.

There were a few of us lost souls wandering around the small, when-in-session population two thousand student college over the holidays, but not many. Most people had somewhere to go, people to see. I was an only child. It looked like this year I'd be with my books this Christmas. Introverted by nature, I'd intuited that my quietness had made my roommate's family uncomfortable over Thanksgiving, and I hadn't been invited back to her home with her over these holidays. I knew I was right about the awkwardness. I'd known it was happening while it was happening, and yet I'd seemed unable to stop the mess.

That was okay. I'd spent most of the time really unsure of what to say to her relatives. No, I grew up mostly in *Kenya. Yes, Kenya. No, I wasn't from Kenya. I was from*

*Pennsylvania originally and then lived in Boston for the rest
of my time in America. It's why I had come back here to go to
school. What? No, my freckles weren't painted on. They ran
in my family. Red hair was a recessive gene. I was pretty
sure.*

I shook my head. Conversations came back to me like
that. All at once and overpowering, as though I had to relive
them each time I thought of them. I hadn't been raised on
small talk. My parents liked serious conversations. We
didn't speak if there was nothing important to say.

"Hey, there, library," a voice called out, and I kept walking. It came from across the street. Someone was saying
something about the library. I didn't look over.

I was on fraternity row. Ten fraternity houses and ten
sorority houses were lined up, one after another, looking
somehow both glamorous and dirty at the same time. I'd not
pledged a Greek organization my freshman year. I could
barely keep up with my classes. I didn't have time to party.
And there was the cost involved. My parents held my purs-
estrings, and they found such organizations to be pointless.
Even if I could have gotten around those two facts, like by
getting a job I didn't have time for because I had to study all
the time, there was the introverted issue.

I avoided this street when school was in session. There
were too many people and too much noise. I shook my head.
I was a junior. This was the first holiday I had to spend
alone. Every other school break, I'd gone home to Boston.
My family didn't even celebrate things. Not really, anyway.
My mother was too concerned with dissecting every little
bit of tradition into its root origin of something to do with
harvest or fertility.

I spent last Christmas alone in my room, reading
mysteries. And... I had to snap out of this funk.

"Hey," that voice again. This time closer as someone's jogging feet caught up with me. "I'm talking to you, library. Stop."

I turned to see who addressed me. I knew few people even for such a small campus, and no one I was familiar with was here over the holidays.

A guy stood behind me on the sidewalk. "Why didn't you stop?"

I blinked. "I'm sorry?"

"When I called out to you, why didn't you stop?"

I still didn't understand. "When did you call out to me?"

I knew better than to talk to strange men on the street. But this one wore a sweatshirt that said SPiI on it, indicating he was a brother in what I thought was referred to as the SPiI house. Sigma Pi Iota, and the students called it SPiI. My roommate, Molly, always said they were the best looking guys on campus. Apparently, their house was hard to get into. Most of the men who wanted to pledge the house were rejected, with brotherhood offered to legacies—meaning they had a father or a brother or a grandfather who had been brothers in a SPiI house somewhere—and very select few members of the community.

Molly's long-term boyfriend was a member of Delta Kappa Iota, or DKI. Apparently the two houses didn't like each other. And it was sort of weird that she thought the SPiI boys were so good looking when she dated a DKI. I didn't spend much time thinking about these things. But now that I thought about it, did the fraternities not like each other because they both used the Iota in their names? And who named them anyway?

Still, all of those thoughts aside, I wasn't going to stand on the street and talk to this stranger in the cold. Wasn't he freezing? He was just in a sweatshirt and jeans and a pair of sneakers. I was chilled to the bone in my winter coat.

"Just before." He turned slightly to point to the white house with the SPiI letters on the front. "I called out to you from there."

Oh, yes. He'd been yelling from the house. "You said something about the library? You were calling to me? Sorry, I didn't understand. Are you looking for the library? It's not far." I started to turn to point it out, and he laughed, stopping me.

He was sort of... beautiful. Men weren't usually referred to as thus, but he was. Tall, sandy blond hair, and blue eyed. He was tall, so no one would call him dainty or anything, especially with his muscles being so broad. The cleft in his chin really kept him from being feminine looking. And, oh hell, I was staring at him. I looked down at my feet.

"I know where the library is. I'm a senior. I've been a few times. No, I was calling you library."

I stopped looking at my feet to meet his eyes. "Why were you calling me library?"

"Because I didn't know what to call you. I see you going in and out of the library all the time when I'm at my council meetings at the Dean's office. In and out. Over and over. Each week. I started thinking of you as library girl. Shortened it. Library."

Maybe he thought he was charming. He was certainly handsome enough to get the kind of attention from women that would let him think every word out of his mouth was a gift to the female gender.

"I had no way of knowing you called me library in your head or whatever, so it makes sense I wouldn't know to answer to it." Nor did I have any intention of answering to it, ever. "What did you need?"

He put out his hand. "I wanted to say hi. I'm Maven Stone. Nice to meet you."

I stared at his offering before I took it. I did have manners. "Giovanna Amsel."

"Cool name."

I'd always hated it. About half the people who tried to pronounce it got it wrong. My parents called me Vonni and that was fine.

"Well, thanks." I nodded at him. "Was there a particular reason you wanted to say hi? Do you need something?"

He crossed his arms over his chest. Maven, which was also a cool name, must have been getting cold. "I needed something else to call you besides library in my head."

"Well, then." I cleared my throat. My mother was so personable. Her classes hung on every word she spoke. I never knew what to say, and this was so bizarre I didn't have a good answer. "Now you do. Nice to meet you, Maven."

I started to leave, and he spoke again. "It's cold out here."

"Yes, so you should probably go inside and put on a coat."

He raised both his eyebrows. "Or you could come inside with me, where it's warm, and I could make us coffee. Or something stronger if you'd like."

Coffee I loved. I didn't drink alcohol because I had a million reasons not to become intoxicated. But I wasn't going inside with him, either way. "Thank you for the offer, but no thank you."

I'd never been in a fraternity house, and I wasn't going into one, alone, with a guy who yelled at me on the street. That sounded like the beginning of a novel where the frat boy murdered a girl, no one knew what happened to her, and some detective had to figure it out. It was even a perfect set up. My bereaved parents wouldn't hear what happened to me for six months when they return from being the first people to learn the language of a previously-untouched-by-the-modern-world people to try to get answers about why their daughter was dead.

Although I had a hard time picturing Maven as a murderer. He had kindness in his eyes. Most people didn't.

"Hey," someone shouted from the SPiI porch. "What are you doing?"

A dark-haired guy wearing jeans and a t-shirt and, I realized as he got closer, no shoes ran towards us. There was snow on the ground. What was the matter with these people? Didn't they have any sense? This wasn't Harvard, but test scores to get in here had to be high. They couldn't be this dumb.

"Hey." The dark-haired, green-eyed guy grinned. "What's going on? Saw you two out here. Maven. Giovanna, hi."

He knew my name? I tried to place if I had ever met this person before in my life. He was as tall as Maven and also buff. Did they work out all the time? He had an earring in his left ear and ink visible just barely through his shirtsleeves. His face was long and his cheekbones high. I really couldn't remember ever seeing his face before.

"Oh, so you two know each other?" Maven looked between us.

"No, I don't think so." Maybe I should have pretended, but I didn't have a clue who the new addition to this odd conversation was.

The dark-haired newbie clutched his heart. "Ouch.

Beautiful redhead doesn't remember meeting me. I am mortally wounded."

Maven rolled his eyes. "Chance Montgomery, meet Giovanna Amsel. Giovanna, my fraternity brother, Chance. He is our pledge master. He's good with faces and names. I don't think he ever forgets anyone once he's met them or learned their name. It's kind of a requirement for the job."

That was interesting. I was going to have to learn more about this at some point. When I was alone on my computer.

"We met, once," Chance spoke again. He had, if my ears didn't deceive me, a New York accent. With Maven, I hadn't detected any noticeable regional inflections at all. Chance's wasn't strong, but it was there. "Or not met, per se. But you were in my psychology class two years ago. You sat toward the back of the room in the corner, to the left. I sat, mostly, in the center. You didn't talk much, but when you did, you were always right."

I had hated that class with a passion. I was an English major, and psychology certainly helped with the study of English, particularly Freud who was used more in studying English literature now than he was in actual psychology. The problem I had was I'd spent so much time around college professors in my life. I'd become adept at determining who was the real deal. I could tell who was passionate about their subject, anxious to teach, happy to really make themselves relevant in their field versus the ones who just wanted to be worshiped by a bunch of twenty somethings too enamored with their teachers to know their instructors were mediocre at best and usually on an ego trip.

Or maybe I should spend more time in psychology classes to get a grasp on my own negativity.

There was nothing more important than a good teacher.

That psychology class? Professor King had not been a good one.

I had to speak. I'd been quiet too long. "I'm not good with people. I don't usually remember those I don't spend a lot of time with. Um, faces sometimes more than names. Sorry, please don't be offended. I'm better with books." I looked at Maven. "Hence the library."

He smiled, a real grin. Maybe we'd just had a moment, some kind of inside joke. Okay, time for me to leave.

"Did you invite her inside? It's cold out here."

I pointed at his feet. "Particularly because you're not wearing shoes?"

"What?" He stared down at his feet. "Damn, no I'm not."

"Did you seriously not know you weren't wearing shoes?" Maven shoved Chance's shoulder. "Pick your head up from the books for ten minutes and join us here in the real world please before you lose sense of reality altogether."

Chance pointed at Maven. "Thinks he's my father. You have such pretty hair, Giovanna. Couldn't miss you in the back of that room."

"Oh, thank you." I took another step away. I didn't know if I was pretty or not. It was hard to tell, really. My parents didn't tell me I was. They were more interested in intellectual pursuits, and my dyslexia, which they had taught me to deal with, had put a real stop to their plans for me to be the next Einstein or whatever it was they wanted.

Guys didn't look at me much. Or maybe I didn't look at them. I'd had one boyfriend, briefly, in high school, when we'd moved to Boston. He hadn't talked much either. We were two introverts who spent a lot of time unsure of what to do with the other one. The sex had been great. But that had been about it.

I did miss sex. Two years without it. Why was I thinking about this now?

"Well, it was nice to meet you two." When in doubt, I could call upon my manners. "I'd better get going, and you'd both better get inside. It is, as we've said multiple times, cold out here."

Just then, a car pulled down the street, stopping next to us. It was a red SUV with tinted windows. The passenger side window rolled down. A third guy's face became visible. He was dark haired but not as dark as Chance.

"Hey, are we having some sort of event here on the street? What is the matter with the three of you? It's cold out here. Oh, look you're talking to Giovanna."

Okay, I really didn't know this person at all. No noticeable accent. This was a small school, but I'd always assumed most people had no idea who I was. And I'd been pretty much fine with that. "I—"

Maven interrupted me. "You don't know him either? Wow. You two really don't make much of an impression on pretty girls. Me? She'll never forget her introduction to me. This is Banyan Iburgess. Banyan, you seem to know Giovanna?"

"Sure." He smiled. "She runs the literary magazine. You hired me. Granted, over email. I'm doing the cover this year. The artwork."

"Oh." Now that he'd said the name. Yes, I knew his work. "You are so talented."

Banyan's face lit up like a Christmas tree at my compliment. "You think so?"

"There'll be no shutting him up now." Chance laughed. "Watch out, Giovanna. He loves fans."

Banyan rolled his eyes. "Don't listen to him. He's jealous. Straight As boy there can't hold a paintbrush to save his life."

Maven pointed at the house. "Seriously, come inside."

"Sorry, but I just met you three." When in doubt, honesty worked. "And I know better than to go into a fraternity house with three guys I just met, particularly in light of the fact that the campus is basically empty right now. Don't be insulted, please. I wouldn't go into an apartment either. Or a car."

Maven nodded. "It's smart. But I'd like to point out that there has not been one—not one—sexual assault accusation made against any member of SPiI since I've been a member. I'm the president now. The guys know my take on this matter."

"No sexual assault by any member or none reported?" Oh hell, why had I said that? Every once in a while, despite my introverted nature and my just general shyness, or sometimes just my lack of liking anyone around, I couldn't seem to keep my mouth shut.

Maven's smile was slow. "I really like you. I do. I mean, I kind of thought I would. There's something about you. And you're not afraid either, which is...yeah." He ran a hand through his blond hair. "Okay. If any of my brothers or pledges were to disrespect a woman, the police would be making two arrests that night. One for whatever it was the asshat did, and the second would be me for the beating I'd give the guy. We are all accountable to each other and for each other. That's how this works."

"Well, come on." Chance shrugged. "We're here right now because we fucked up. She has to know that. The incident was widely known around campus. She has reason to think if we could let that happen, we could make other questionable choices."

The incident? I was going to have to text Molly. She'd explain it to me. For now, I was going to keep quiet. I'd said enough. More than, actually.

"There is a difference between a pledge joke—poorly thought out and executed horrendously—gone wrong and sexual assault. They hung underwear from a flagpole. It wasn't..."

"Enough," Banyan interrupted Maven and Chance. "Yes, we all know why we're here cleaning up the campus this holiday instead of being at home doing whatever it is we do there. Giovanna, I approve of the thought. Don't go into any fraternity houses alone. Except mine. Mine is safe. But, yes, don't do that until you believe me. Do you have a car?"

I didn't, actually. It was weird for people on this campus not to have one. My father had told me if I made good grades, I could have one for after graduation. I wasn't sure I would need it. My plan was to go to graduate school in New York City. I wouldn't need a car there. Not that I'd told them that, yet. I tended to hold back on informing my parents about my plans until I absolutely had to. This course of action minimized the amount I had to speak to them about my life.

"No."

Banyan pouted dramatically at me through his car window. "Too bad. I was going to suggest you go get your car and you could follow me to dinner. We could all do that. They'd get in this car. You in your own. Then everyone is safe and happy."

"It's three o'clock." Did they eat dinner at three o'clock? "Or were we going to drive in this hypothetical plan two hours away to eat?"

Banyan sat up straight. "Oh, I can think of a lot of

places I'd like to eat two hours from here. Come on, Giovanna. I'm totally not scary."

I laughed. This really had become amusing. That didn't mean I was getting in the car with them. "You guys have a great afternoon. I'm going to get going now. Good luck with whatever this is you have to do to make up for your incident. This has been unexpected."

I turned my back on them and walked away. When I finally turned the corner, I didn't feel their gazes on me anymore. My pulse raced, and I tried to pretend it wasn't because I'd had the attention of three hot guys for a few minutes. They were probably bored and feeding off each other's energy. Maven had decided it would be fun to shout at me across the street. Chance had come to see what Maven was doing. And Banyan stumbled on us all. I was the only female around for them to flirt with for a while.

Yep, that was it. I sent a text to Molly. She'd been my closest friend since freshman year. Even if lately she spent a lot more time with her boyfriend than me. I had other friends, but most of them were like me—they studied and went to the movies. She was the only one I knew who actually had anything to do with Greek life on campus by dating her DKI boyfriend. The Greeks pretty much stayed to themselves. Sorority girls dated fraternity guys. They partied, studied, and had drama all the time with each other.

I just met Maven, Chance, and Banyan. I didn't use last names. There couldn't be more than one guy on campus with their first names. *They're here doing something for some sort of incident?*

It took almost no time to get the response. *!!! Yes! The SPiI guys got in trouble. Their pledges got caught putting underwear up the main flagpole in the quad. Stupid prank* *and stupid to get caught. They have to do three hundred hours of community service by June or they lose their charter. The SPiI board was pissed. That's Chance's fault. He's their pledge master. But it all comes down to Maven's responsibility. Banyan's not off the hook too—he's their social chair. They're all responsible. There are like 12 of them on the board. They're all there. Wanted to get a jump on their punishment.*

Well that was interesting. It explained the underwear comment. And why they were here. I shook my head. It was like a different world or something. What would possess grown men to run underwear up a flagpole?

I kept walking, and my phone pinged again.

If I wasn't with R.J., I'd want to be with Chance. He is hot. How are you? I'm sorry. I should have thought to invite you again. Do you want to come to my house?

She lived three hours away. The invite was, at this point, fruitless. I wasn't going to get on a bus to make it for Christmas Eve dinner. Not to mention, R.J. was going to be there, and I couldn't stand him. He had mean eyes. Direct contrast, in fact, to Maven's. R.J. seemed angry at the world.

I'd been alone here for a week and would be through New Year's. Everyone would get back to campus before January 7th for classes to start.

I'm okay. Thanks for the invite. See you next year.

I put my phone in my pocket. She was right. Chance was hot. But then so were Maven and Banyan. I wouldn't throw any of them out of my bed.

When I'd gotten up this morning, the last thing I'd thought would happen was spending time talking to SPiI brothers on the street. Life was funny sometimes.

TWO

A blaring alarm meant to raise the dead sent me darting from sound sleep to total alertness all at once. It was two in the morning, Christmas Day, and the fire alarm in my mostly empty dorm blared warning. I grabbed my shoes and ran for the door. We'd done a fire drill upon moving in during the fall, but I'd hardly paid attention.

Okay, I had to think. Some things were basic. In a fire alarm situation, the elevators weren't going to work. I ran for the stairs. Fortunately, I lived on the fourth floor and not the tenth. I took the stairs two at a time. A few bangs here and there echoed as the few others staying in the dorm for the holiday exited. I didn't know any of them personally, but the Residential Advisor, Emily, had told me that there were six others.

The closer I got to the ground floor, the more I smelled smoke. My heart raced so fast I could hear it in my ears. I really, really hoped it wasn't blocking the door to the street. I pulled my shirt over my nose, bent my head, and kept running. When I got to the lobby, I found the hallway clear and the smoke coming from the wall vents. What did that mean? Smoke traveled upward. Was there a fire in the base-ment? The laundry room? I'd let the firemen find out. I just ran out the door.

There were two others out there, and fortunately within minutes, a total of seven of us stood on the street staring up at the building as the firemen arrived. They moved us back.

And then there was noise. Chaos.

I still held my shoes. I'd carried them all the way down, never putting them on. I bent over and shoved my sneakers on my feet. I made myself breathe. There had been an actual fire. That hadn't been a hypothetical thing.

Earlier, I'd pictured my family trying to find my frat boy murderer. This time, I pictured them receiving the tragic news that their daughter had been burned to death. Was it negligence? Would they hire a top litigator to sue the school? Run fire safety lessons in my name?

"Hey!"

I turned around to see Maven, Chance, and Banyan rushing toward me. It was Chance who'd called out. "Are you okay? We heard sirens."

They weren't alone. A crowd of guys wearing SPiI shirts formed behind them as well as some guys wearing the same plain gray sweatshirt, obviously all meant to look the same. That was bizarre. It was Christmas Day. What were they all doing here?

I blinked trying to bring myself to the here and now. Stress always made me shut down. "There's a fire."

"Shit." Maven looked around. "Guys. Okay, we're only going to be in the way here. We need to leave so these people can do their jobs without worrying about having to save our stupid asses from falling debris or ashes or anything that might come off the building. Come on. Back to the house. Tomorrow, we'll figure out ways to help. Into the cars. Go. Now."

Maven must really hold a lot of sway. Everyone behind him started moving except the guys in gray sweatshirts. They stayed still. Chance whistled loudly. "You, too, children. Back to the house."

The guys in gray sweatshirts walked in a single line back to their cars. Banyan touched my back. "Hey, pretty girl, you okay?"

I snapped out of it. "Yes. Sorry. You should go. I have to stay here till this is over."

Maven put his hand on my arm. "Why do you have to stay here?"

"I live here." Why wasn't this clear? "Pretty much everything that belongs to me in the world is inside of there."

"You staying here, freezing, in pajamas isn't going to help that." Chance tugged the end of my braid. That was when it occurred to me what I was wearing. Not that it particularly mattered in this situation, but I'd never meant to leave the dorm in my blue flannel pajamas and a white tank top. The wind picked up and snow dripped slowly from the sky hitting my exposed arms. I stared down at myself. Oh this was bad. Any second my shirt was going to be total see through, and as soon as my adrenaline wore off, I was going to be freezing.

I nodded. Chance was probably right. "I don't have any choice, really. My wallet is inside there. I can't go anywhere without it. I can't even get a hotel room. My parents are unreachable. I..." I stopped talking. I didn't want to cry. I would physically not let those tears fall. I sucked them in. Hard. I would simply not speak until I was sure I wasn't going to break down. It was hard, but I'd successfully managed it before. Nothing was ever made better by letting them out.

"Here." Maven took off his coat and wrapped me in it. It was black and leather. So he did have a coat. That would be funny, if I could say that aloud. But I couldn't speak. Not yet. Tears were too close. "You're not going to stay out here for hours—and it could be hours—for them to figure this out. You'll come with us. I know you have that thing about frat houses. You'll be safe. I promise. We'll stay with you, all three of us, and there are women in the house right now. Ridge's sister is here for the holiday. And two of the guys have girlfriends."

I wanted to argue. Earlier, I'd been quite adamant that I wasn't going into SPiI anytime soon without friends with me. But these guys were here, and I was alone in the world. Chance squeezed my hand. "Come on. Let's get you somewhere other than here."

I let him bring me along. I wasn't even worried. Maybe my lack of worry was caused by the shock of the evening, or maybe it was just that there was something about these three that said they wouldn't hurt me. They'd heard sirens, and they'd left their beds to come see if they could help.

I was on autopilot. Banyan scooted in next to me in the backseat of a blue car, not his red SUV from earlier. It smelled new. Maven got in the driver's side, and Chance in the front passenger seat.

Banyan had brown eyes. I hadn't noticed them before. He'd been too far away for me to see them. They had a little bit of green in the center.

"That was scary as hell, I bet." He squeezed my fingers. "I've never been in a fire."

"I have," Maven added from the front seat as he pulled the car onto the street and away from the scene behind us.

He didn't add any more. Did that mean he hadn't been scared? Or that he had been?

Chance turned around to regard me from the front seat. "Are you hungry?"

"No, thank you." I shook my head. "Wait. Please stop. You should take me back. You don't even know me. Really, you shouldn't be putting yourselves out for me."

This didn't make sense. People were inherently mean. If there was anything I'd learned over the years of traveling through hundreds of different cultural studies at my parents' side, it was that humanity was basically the same everywhere. And all of it pretty much sucked.

Banyan let go of my hand to rub my back. "So far, all we've done is put you in a car. Oh and Maven gave you a coat. Got to that faster than me. We'd do this for anyone."

"There are six other people who are currently unable to get in their dorm rooms."

Chance nodded. "Good point." He picked up his phone and started texting. "I'm going to ask Ridge and Greg to go over and make sure everyone has somewhere to go. You're right, Giovanna, we were very focused on you. Lots of reasons why that might be." He looked at Maven. "Okay if I say the directive comes from you?"

"Absolutely." Maven spoke and then pulled into the driveway of SPiI as Chance put down the phone. "Any of them who want to come here are welcome. We've got lots of food. After I'm gone, they can run this any way they want to, but until I've graduated, this place stays the house we pledged. Yes?"

Chance nodded once. "Absolutely. On board all the way, Mr. President." Maven smirked at Chance who turned back to me. "We're really not doing anything much here. It's not like you're going to owe us some giant favor."

Banyan winked at me. "Just a couple of small ones?"

Maven groaned. "She's not ready for jokes yet. She's still half convinced we worship Satan in the basement."

I hadn't actually thought that. I smiled. "Do you all don robes and cover yourselves in cow's blood?"

There were religions that did that sort of thing. I'd seen it. That was beside the point. They were right. They'd been nothing but nice to me, and I was protesting something I actually needed—a place to stay until I could go back to my dorm.

I wasn't going to look a gift horse in the mouth.

It was Christmas. I would, somehow, believe in the goodwill of men, or at least SPiI brothers in this case.

I didn't have my cell phone. If it burned down or was otherwise destroyed in this mess, I was going to be in big trouble. I didn't know my parent's international phone numbers. I would have to call Harvard and get them to deliver them a message.

This was going to be a mess.

"Are you hungry?" Chance asked me again as we got out of the car and headed toward the house. "I had the pledges bake last night."

He held the door for me, and I walked through. Maven and Banyan followed behind me. It was significantly warmer inside the house, and a hissing sound greeted me. It took a second for me to identify the noise as the radiators warming up the old house. The dorms were newer and the heating systems more updated.

The last time I had heard this hissing noise had been in a bed and breakfast in New Hampshire my mother had taken us to when she needed out of the city to finish her paper. I'd read my book and listened to that noise.

I shook my head. Memories were funny. Just a sound of

hissing air could take me to another time and place. Chance was waiting for me to answer. These guys were learning fast I was usually lost in my own mind.

"Um, no. I don't usually eat in the middle of the night."

Maven looked at Banyan. "It is the middle of the night, isn't it?" Banyan shrugged and touched my shoulder while he passed me going down the hall. Maven spoke again. "We are sort of nocturnal here. If we didn't have classes, we might never see daylight. It was hard over the summer to work. I had to completely readjust my body."

"Well, semi adjust it, right?" Chance took off his coat then helped me out of mine. I could certainly have taken Maven's coat off myself, but he beat me to it. I was still staring at the scene in front of me. I never would have thought this house would be so nice. It had a huge central opening that led to two very long staircases. One that went upstairs and one that led to a basement beneath us. It was an open floor plan so I could see the kitchen to the right and a dining area with a lot of tables and chairs set up for eating to the left.

The carpet was gray, and although I would say that the outside of the house needed a coat of paint—I'd thought it on more than one occasion when I'd walked by, some of the white paint was peeling—the inside was well kept. At least as far as I could see.

"So, you're sure you're not hungry?" Chance asked for the third time.

I shook my head. "No, thank you. Did you say you had the pledges baking? Do they just do whatever you tell them to do?"

"They do." He winked at me. "If they want to be a brother here. Well, I'm hungry. I want a cookie."

He passed by me to the kitchen. I still had a question so

I addressed it to Maven. "And this extends so far that they are all here with you instead of with their families over the holidays?"

"They got to go home for a bit and had to come back. The punishment was meant to hurt. But they got us in trouble, and they know they're not supposed to do that."

Maven nodded toward the kitchen, and I followed him there. "Sorry to press, but what if their families objected?"

"A huge number of them are alumni. They won't object. They want their sons here with me, becoming brothers of this house. The ones who aren't have to be educated about how this goes. It's one year of their life. I didn't miss Christmas my freshman year, but I didn't run undergarments up a flagpole in front of the Dean. Actions have consequences. I'm here, too. I've been here, and I let them go home for a bit. They're spending Christmas at a food kitchen later today. Not because the school wants that, but because I want them to."

Chance swallowed his cookie, offered me one, which I declined with a shake of my head, and spoke again. "Some of this is about taking kids who have just come out of high school and helping to shape them into men. We're not perfect. We make a lot of mistakes. I am hugely flawed. But as brothers in this house, we walk respectable lines. That's how it goes."

"Oh." I must have been tired because I didn't think about what I said before I uttered my next words. "Outside of this house, what people say is that SPiI has the hot guys." I covered my mouth. "It's late. I apologize."

Maven grinned at me, slowly. "Is that so, Giovanna? We have that rep?"

"I..." I shook my head. There was no way to make that better. "Like you haven't heard that yourself."

Chance winked at me. "He has. And thanks. We'll take it. But that's just a matter of genes. We don't actually choose our brothers during rush week based on how they look. GPA in high school. Extracurricular. Whether or not they're legacies. Their interest in the house. Guess we just lucked out that the ladies like us, too."

Banyan hurried back into the room. "Heard some of that. Chance has no shortage of confidence. Come on. I did a cursory look through the rooms. Maven's is the cleanest. You can sleep in there."

"Oh." My hand went to my throat. "I can't do that."

Maven took one of the cookies. "You can. I'll sleep elsewhere."

"That's not what I was worried about." I actually wouldn't mind Maven sleeping in there with me. Or not sleeping as the case might be. These guys were seriously hot. But that didn't mean I was going to actually do it. This was a small campus. And academia was a small community. I couldn't let my parents' colleagues ever hear a bad rumor about me. One and a half more years and I'd be on my own, sort of. Unless I followed the plan to go to graduate school...

"Then what were you worried about? I even changed the sheets this morning."

Banyan grinned. "He thinks to do those things. I never do. I'd really have to clean before you got in my room."

"Paint everywhere. He redoes the walls constantly," Chance added.

"I don't want to put you out of your room."

Maven held my eye contact for a second. "It won't be a problem." He nodded toward the hall. "Come on. You should get some rest."

"I don't know if I can sleep." Still, I followed him. The more I knew Maven, the harder it was to tell him no. I'd resisted on the street earlier. Now, however, it was like he assumed authority and so I was sort of giving it to him. I could stop. Except right at this moment, I really didn't want to.

Right before I got to the stairs, Chance called to me. "Goodnight, Giovanna. We're going to keep an ear toward what's happening at your dorm. When you wake up, we'll know something."

Banyan nodded. "And we love breakfast. So, you'll get some of that, too. Night, beautiful."

"Um, goodnight and thank you." Breakfast? Didn't they say they were up all night? Maybe that was their last meal of the day? How did they get to class?

Maven's room was in the center of the hallway upstairs. I knew this place was huge, but I hadn't realized just how big. There was another staircase at the end of the hallway leading to a third floor. Who got to live up there?

Maybe it was just attic space. Maven had dressed his bed in black sheets and a black comforter. His walls had a variety of printed artwork, framed, around the room. He had a desk, which was neat with folders stacked all around, and his closet door was closed. Banyan hadn't been wrong. Maven was neat. Much more so than I was.

"You really don't have to do this. I could sit and wait at one of the tables."

"No way, library. You need to sleep off that adrenaline. Or cry maybe. You were trying not to in the car. You can do that alone."

I swallowed. "How did you know that?"

"I'm good at reading people. So, toothbrush at the top of my dresser." I hadn't noticed the dresser, took me a second to realize it was the back of the desk. That was sort of an ingenious use of space. "Grab one of my t-shirts from the closet. Sleep. Or don't. But we'll leave you alone." His phone beeped, and he pulled it out of his pants. "None of the others wanted to come. They all went to other places. Ridge is coming back. Good of you to think of them, though. What do you need? What can I get you?"

One of the pictures on the walls caught my attention. "I have this print, too. John Abdul. I love his work."

Maven moved until he stood next to me. He smelled like soap. "You do? Yes, I like old bookstores. They're few and far between these days. They always have things like that, in addition to cool books. I looked up the print. He's apparently really famous in the new wave of American folk art."

The lines of the man playing guitar on the fence coincided with the bars of the prison behind him. "He is. I've met him. A few times."

He was nice to me. That was something I didn't forget easily.

"You have?" Maven side-eyed me. "When?"

"He teaches at Harvard. Sometimes. Takes the job when he's run through his savings. He's not good with money but whatever. He's a genius, and the university never turns down a few classes from him."

Maven turned to face me entirely. "You spent time at Harvard?"

"My parents are professors there. I mean, right now they're in India. Trying to reach a tribe that refuses contact with the outside world. They might get killed by poison darts. It's a real thing. Look it up."

He held up his hands. "I didn't doubt you."

"Every once in a while, I get accused of making that up." I had to stop being so defensive.

Maven took my hand in his and rubbed the center of my

palm. "Bet you've had a really interesting life. I'd like to hear your stories. Tomorrow."

"My parents have had a lot of important discoveries. I used to kind of come along." I should pull my hand out of his. I was really letting these guys touch me, which was unusual. I was big on personal space. The thing was... I liked it. "What do your parents do?"

Maven nodded and looked away before regaining my eye contact in what I could only call a hard stare. "My father sold illegal junk bonds before he went to jail. He's doing the last of a five year stint right now in a federal prison. My mother is a prosecutor in New York City, so it was a minor scandal for a while. She didn't know. She's held to that statement the whole time, and sometimes I believe her. Good news is that her family is loaded, so nothing much had to change in our lives despite the old man's nefarious behavior and life behind bars."

He had just given me a ton of information, and I should be overwhelmed by it. It took a long time, usually, to get that kind of personal story from someone. It almost seemed like Maven was challenging me. Would I look away? Would I be horrified? Judgmental? Beneath his hard gaze, there was something else. Pain. He hid it well beneath the take me or leave me attitude, but boy oh boy, it was there.

"That had to be a lot to deal with while you were applying to college."

Maven blinked a few times before he smiled at me. "Made for a great personal statement for my essay."

"I'm sorry your parents so royally screwed up. Mine sort of forget I'm around sometimes or that I might need anything beyond basic necessities. Like conversation." I smiled at him. "You seem really nice, Maven. Are you? Or is this some sort of be kind to the library girl for a couple days while you're bored?"

He whispered his response. "I'm really nice. But I don't think a lot of people know that, so don't tell. I'm confessing all my secrets to you. *Giovanna*. I can't call you library now that you said it. I like your name too much anyway. What is it about you? I've thought about you a ridiculous amount for not knowing who you were, and since I met you, I've had you on the edge of my mind. Now here you are. Girls don't sleep in my bed. Ever. I never have them up here."

"Oh." I dropped his hand. "I'm sorry. Banyan pushed you into this, didn't he? I mean it. I'll go downstairs and..."

His mouth met mine, not hard but not soft either. Just the right amount of pressure. I closed my eyes and let him. Maven didn't ask for more. He didn't even pull me against him. My body came alive. Buzzing with desire. I was shy in a lot of ways but not sexually. I wanted it. I loved it. I wanted him. Still, I stayed where I was.

Maven stroked one finger down the side of my cheek before he stopped kissing me. Still close to my mouth, he spoke. "Goodnight, Giovanna. Get some sleep. Merry Christmas." He pressed his forehead to mine. "We never asked you. Do you celebrate Christmas?"

"Sort of. My father's family is Jewish. Mom's was Catholic. But they're both sort of agnostic and interested in the history behind the religion rather than the practice itself, except as an intellectual thing." I couldn't believe I was still practically embracing him and talking about the strange ways my family behaved. "It's really just an excuse to eat turkey in my house. How about you?"

He didn't answer for a minute. "In our house, it's an excuse to yell at each other. And go out to eat before returning home to do it again. Never my favorite time. Since

Dad went away, we drop the pretense. I spent last year with Banyan and Chance on Chance's dad's boat in the Caribbean drinking beer. Love that you're here. I really do. Going to back off now." Maven stepped back. "Goodnight."

"Goodnight."

I stood there for a minute after he closed the door, leaving me alone, before I turned back to the Abdul painting. He'd just confessed his family history to me, and I didn't have enough fact to wonder about what the symbols of that painting meant to him. That didn't stop me from doing it though. He had in his room a man strumming a guitar in front of a prison. To me, it had been about finding happiness in dire circumstances.

What did the jail in the painting mean to Maven? Was he inside of it or out when he looked at it?

THREE

I didn't think I would sleep, but Maven's bed was soft, comfortable, and his pillow nice and cool. Sleep dragged me under to a series of weird dreams that had me running from some unknown enemy who chased at my heels. The location kept changing, but the need to flee for my life kept up with me.

Light streamed through the windows when I opened my eyes. The sound downstairs finally pulled me out of my fog. Between the fire and the bad dreams, I'd be a mess if I wasn't used to not sleeping very well. I had a hard time turning off my head. Most of the time I read, since I was alone more often than not in my room. Molly slept with R.J. most nights in his fraternity house.

I'd never imagined spending the night in a fraternity house. And yet... here I was. His bed smelled really good. I took a deep whiff. This was going to be a one time thing, so I really needed to make a memory of it. There was just a way, sometimes, that guys smelled. A purely male scent. It wasn't sweat or cologne. Maybe it was his soap and shampoo. Perhaps Maven washed his hair before he went to bed at night and that was the woodsy, clean aroma that clung to his sheets.

Or maybe I was just obsessed because he'd kissed me. What had that been about? I saw the lines of women who wanted to get in here on Thursday, Friday, and Saturday nights from my dorm room window. With the exception of one house that didn't seem get any attention, every frat on campus was overwhelmed with women wanting to party. SPiI had to turn people away at the door. Why bother with me? Maybe it had just been a moment—we were alone in his bedroom, in the middle of the night, talking about our parents in front of a painting that evoked a reaction in anyone who spent time looking at it. Yes, I was going to go with that.

I was stiff, and I had to pee, which meant I had to go find a bathroom. Shared toilet facilities would be something I wouldn't miss when I was finally out of college. Or at least not having to share them with a whole hallway of people.

I stuck my head out the door. All of the noise I heard was downstairs. Upstairs, the hallway was quiet. I had a lot of questions about this fraternity now that I'd stepped through the doors. How many brothers did they have? What happened after graduation? Did the pledges live here, too?

I made my way down the hall until I found the bathroom, which was surprisingly clean, considering this was a frat house and stereotypically guys were not all that neat. Of course, I'd lived enough unusual places to know that stereotypes were usually incredibly wrong.

It was good to learn something new every day. This morning it was that the upstairs bathroom in SPiI was clean. I wished I had my phone. I'd text Molly what was happening here. She'd never believe I did this. I was

Giovanna, the girl who studied, ran the lit magazine, and went to the movies. Sure, I had friends I did this stuff with, but I didn't go to parties. I didn't even drink. How had I just spent the night at a frat house?

I headed downstairs toward the sounds of conversation. I really didn't know what I was supposed to do now. Could I go back to my dorm?

The kitchen was filled with people eating and laughing. The guys who had been in gray shirts the night before were wearing khaki pants, white collared shirts, red ties, and blue vests. Those had to be the pledges. I'd never noticed people walking around in the same clothes during the regular school year. Maybe this was just something they were doing this week.

Chance sat on the counter, Banyan next to him, and around the sides of the room were four guys I didn't recognize. Two of them had women with them.

I hated this kind of moment. Walking into a room where you hardly knew anyone and having to just... be there. "Hi. Good morning."

Banyan's face lit up. "Giovanna. Hey."

He was dressed the same as he had been the day before, as was Chance. Had they still not been to bed? Did these guys ever sleep?

"Gentlemen," Chance said to the pledges. "Go ahead."

"Good morning, Giovanna. Merry Christmas."

That was right. It was Christmas Day. Sleeping must have addled my brain. "Thank you. Merry Christmas to all of you."

"They're all getting ready to leave," Chance informed me. "They are going to help people more needy than themselves and remember how fortunate they are to be so privileged that they can go making mistakes like getting caught putting underwear up a flagpole. Go now, all of you. Be back in four hours, and then you can leave. Mommy and Daddy, or whatever version of that you have, will be glad to see you. Scoot."

"Thank you, pledge master." They spoke in unison again before they lined up in a straight line and left the house. They certainly had to do some interesting things before they got to wear three letters across their chest.

"Giovanna, this is Ridge. Tom. Ben. Ridge's sister Eleanor, and Tom's girlfriend Patty. Everyone, Giovanna."

Hellos were said around the room before each one of them exited. I hoped it wasn't because of me, but I didn't really see how it could be. I hadn't done anything. Had I?

Ridge turned on his way out. "We'll be back for New Years. You guys are better men than me. I'm not facing my mother if I don't show up today."

Chance laughed. "Did you see the pledges faces when I said they could go after the food kitchen? I think they were sort of shocked."

"Completely. Have a good one." Ridge waved over his shoulder.

So maybe it wasn't me. They were already all on their way out.

Banyan nudged Chance. "Gentle reminder that pledge Agarwal is Hindu. His family is vegetarian. So…"

Chance nodded fast, clearing his throat. "I know. And we have company. Sorry, Giovanna. Some pledge things have to be secret."

I shook my head. "No worries." I would obviously have to keep a lot of my questions to myself. I was used to sort of being on the outside of things looking in. This wouldn't be different. And besides, it wasn't like I was ever really going to be here again to have any questions about what they would be doing that would require Chance to remember that one of them was a vegetarian. Were they making a dinner?

"Did you sleep okay?" Banyan walked over and pulled me into a hug. He had strong arms, and I liked the hug, which was unusual.

I nodded. "Sure. I need to thank Maven for the use of his room. And I should probably go see if I can find out about my dorm. I..."

I never got to finish what I was going to say. The door to the house opened, and Maven strode in. "Oh good, you're up."

Banyan didn't let me go, which made seeing Maven kind of tricky. "Hi. Thank you so much for your room. You can have it back now."

"No worries," Maven answered, crossing to the fridge. Banyan finally let go of me just as Chance jumped off the counter and came over to hug me, too. Was this a Christmas thing, or were they just both huggers?

Chance smelled like coffee, and my ever present need for caffeine hit me hard. Did they have any? I didn't have my wallet, so walking across campus to get some was pointless. The coffee cart was probably not open on Christmas anyway.

He rubbed the back of my head for a second before he let me go.

Maven took a long sip of some orange juice he must have poured in a glass while I'd been figuring out the hugging thing. "Okay, so the deal with your dorm is that someone set a fire in the laundry room last night. Fortunately, it was just the basement that burned. Sprinklers put most of it out. The building will need to be renovated and fixed a bit. But it will be safe to be inside of it, living there, when school picks back up on January 7th. I managed to convince them that the few students living there needed to be allowed in to get their stuff. Emails are going out to the rest of the college community today."

Banyan patted Maven on the back. "My boy here could convince native Alaskans they wanted to buy snow."

"Thank you. I appreciate that. I can go now?" I headed for the door, and Chance grabbed my arm. "In your sneakers and Maven's shirt while it's twenty degrees outside? I'll drive you."

He was right. Heat infused my cheeks. I really needed to start thinking clearly. "Thanks."

I seemed to be saying that a lot. I was going to have to come up with some way to repay these guys for their kindness. My bank account was low. My parents needed to put some more money into it. They'd insisted they would remember to do so despite being in the middle of nowhere, potentially ducking from poisoned darts. I was going to have to get a job soon if they didn't. While I wasn't opposed to working and wouldn't mind the independence, school was hard for me. I didn't study all the time for fun. I had to really spend time on every subject I took. Dyslexia didn't prevent me from doing anything, and I'd certainly learned to compensate over the years, but it did make some things significantly harder.

"You're welcome."

"Oh." Banyan pulled off his sweatshirt. "Here have this." He started to hand it to me and then stopped. "Not this one. Hold on I'll get another one."

I didn't want him putting himself out. "That's okay. I'll be fine."

"No, seriously. Wait a second. Be right back." Banyan tore up the stairs.

"He can't give you the one he had on because it has our letters on it. The Sigma Pi Iota. Only women who have been officially lettered by the house can wear them. A guy puts up his girlfriend or wife or fiancé for consideration. There's a whole vote and then a big ceremony."

That sounded sort of intense. "You guys have a lot of rules you have to follow, don't you?"

"We self-impose them. Keeps what we value important, keeps the ceremonies meaning something. The brother-hood. The legacy of it all," Maven answered for Chance.

"It matters to us," Chance answered. "And it continues to matter to the alumni who are brothers here. When they are asked about their college experience, they talk a lot about this time. They like the networking and still the sense of belonging. Five years ago when the college talked about eliminating Greek life on campus, three quarters of the alumni threatened to pull their money donations. So that was obviously the end of that. My father and brother still love it. I get that it looks funny from the outside. But from the inside, it's something else I think."

Banyan rushed down the stairs holding a black, paint-splattered sweatshirt. "It's clean. I mean, it's always going to have paint on it. But I just washed it."

I loved it. Instantly. There were so many dots of colors on the black cotton sweatshirt that it almost looked like it had been made to look that way purposefully. "Thank you. I'll take good care of it. I'll wash it before I give it back."

I'd have to find a laundromat since the one in my dorm was going to be out of order for a while, but I would get it done.

"No, keep it. I mean as long as you want. Don't worry about getting it back any time soon or anything. It'll keep you warm."

I took it from him, our hands touching for one second in the exchange. Banyan was adorable. There was no other way to think about it. My cheeks felt warm again. Was I going to blush every time I was near these guys?

"You obviously paint in it."

He one-shoulder shrugged. "I can paint in anything."

Maven looked between us, not speaking, but I felt his gaze following us intently. I took a deep breath. "Thank you, Banyan, for the shirt." I pulled it on over my head. It was huge on me and smelled like laundry detergent. It really would be warm. "I'm not good at accepting generosity or gifts. You three have been so nice to me. I will find a way to pay it back. I promise."

"No need," Banyan answered. "We like having you here, actually. You've never come to our parties, right? I don't think there's enough alcohol in the world to make me forget seeing you."

Maven groaned. "And he pulls out the cheese."

Banyan rolled his eyes. "You just wish you had thought of that."

"Come on." Chance took my hand. "Let's get you back in your dorm before the powers that be change their mind or some red tape alters things."

I let him lead me away. What was it about this place that always made me feel like I had eyes following my every move? I turned slightly to glance over my shoulder. This time, I actually did; both Maven and Banyan watched me depart. I smiled at them, suspecting it looked awkward when I did.

"Bye." I'd almost forgotten to say it. I would have to get Banyan back his shirt. Otherwise, I wasn't sure if I would ever see them again.

OTHER THAN HAVING to walk the four flights of stairs—
or rather run them since everything Chance did seemed to
be at full speed—instead of taking the elevator, I found my
room much as I'd left it. I walked inside and looked around.
Everything was fine. I let out a breath I didn't know I'd held.

Chance walked in after me. "The rooms in this building
are big. I kept picturing my freshman year dorms. I forgot
that they get bigger when you get older. Only the incoming
crew has to suffer."

That was true. We'd lived practically on top of each
other, and my roommate had hated me. She wanted to be
loud and drunk all the time. When she'd started pledging a
sorority half way through our first semester, she'd all but
vanished, sleeping either at the sorority house or at one of
her sisters' rooms. I think we'd both been glad she'd
done that.

But then I'd met Molly in the student lounge, and we'd
hit it off. She'd been my roommate ever since. Only in the
last year had she had R.J., which had changed things. That
was okay. Life was full of change. I had to roll with it.

"My freshman year roommate's name is Miranda
Woods. She's in Mu Gamma Pi. Do you know her?"

I don't know why I asked, exactly. I just sort of wanted
to know if he was pals with Miranda. I rarely disliked
anyone as much as I did her.

The few times she did come back to the room, it was to
take my clothes without asking, and I never got them back.
And she was always such a mess.

"Sure." He didn't comment more but looked around.
"Oh, Maven has that on his wall, too."

I looked where he pointed. "Yes. We talked about it last night."

Chance was so quiet right now. He'd been really chatty in the SPiI house and on the street. Had I done something wrong? "You know he doesn't let girls sleep in his room. I mean, ever. Not one girl the whole time he's been here."

Okay. "It was really nice of him. Of all of you. I'd have been lost last night. You're truly my heroes."

He spun to face me, a grin on his face. "I always wanted to be a hero, but I'm slacking in the hero department. Maven gave you his coat, and you slept in his bed. Banyan has now partially dressed you."

I shook my head. "Not a competition. You were all there. And you seriously helped me. Plus the ride over here right now."

Chance didn't comment and instead walked over to my bookshelf, looking at what I had on it. My room was pretty generic. I had the same comforter I'd had for three years, a blue plain blanket that wasn't too warm or too cold. I didn't own too many clothes. I kept my side mostly tidy. It was my bookshelf that was the most interesting to me. I loved books. Devoured them. I could read a book a day if I didn't have homework.

I grabbed my cell phone. It was where I'd left it charging in the wall. Molly had blown up my messages. I did a quick scan. She must not know about the fire yet. She was mostly complaining about R.J. He'd stood her up last night. I'd text her later.

Instead, I looked up a local hotel and dialed the number. This was going to hurt, and I was going to have to use the emergency credit card to pay for the room. I didn't want to end college in debt, and so far, I'd been very good about not running up charges I couldn't pay for. My question about whether I needed a part time job had basically been answered. To pay for this mess, I was going to have to get one.

The woman answered on the other end, and I listened to her greeting before I spoke. "Hi, yes, I'm hoping you have a room free from now until January 7th."

"Hold one second please, my computer is running a little slowly."

I cleared my throat. I was thirsty. "That's fine. Happy to wait."

Chance shook his head at me. "What are you doing?"

I covered the mouthpiece on my cell. "Getting a hotel room."

"Why?" He put his hands on his hips.

"I need somewhere to sleep. My parents are in India, and they rented our home in Boston out to three students for the year. I've literally got nowhere to go." I thought I had made that clear the night before? Maybe Chance hadn't been listening.

Chance groaned. "Hang up."

"What? No." I turned my back on him. The woman was speaking again.

"How many people will the room be for?"

"Just me," I responded.

Chance touched my arm to get my attention. "Seriously, Giovanna, you'll stay with us. It's just going to be Maven, Banyan, and myself in there from now until school starts back up. You've seen we're not bad guys. Come stay with us."

I shook my head at him. "Chance, you can't possibly want that. I'm basically a stranger."

"Sure. But I'm pretty sure we're going to be... friends." Why had he paused before he said that word? "Please.

Come on. I'm not going to let you go stay by yourself at that hotel. I've been there. Have you? Crummy neighborhood. I'll worry for the next fourteen days. You'll have to put up with me texting you every two hours to check on you."

My mind stuttered. Was he for real with this? "You don't have my cell number."

That was probably the most asinine answer I could give him. In the meantime, I was being rude to the woman on the phone. "I'm sorry, ma'am, I'm going to have to call you back. My apologies."

I disconnected the call. It was Christmas, and that woman was working. I had so just not made her day better.

"Giovanna, what's the problem? Come stay with us. It'll be fun. If it isn't, leave."

He made it seem so simple.

"I can't keep putting Maven out of his bed."

"You don't have to. You can sleep in my room. I even cleaned it up last night while you were sleeping. To be clear, it wasn't dirty or paint splattered like Banyan's can get. Although I think he cleaned, too. I have papers everywhere. I subscribe to my own organization system that only I can understand. It works for me. But there were papers."

I rubbed my eyes. "Chance, for goodness' sake, you shouldn't have to leave your room either."

He held up two fingers. "I have two beds. So I don't have to leave. We can be roomies."

I supposed I should be freaked out by that suggestion, but I wasn't. A warm flush traveled through me. The whole night with Chance? "I feel like I'd still be putting you out."

"I'm not all that nice, Giovanna. I mean, I'm not mean. But I don't go around offering up my bedroom to every person who needs one. I like you. I liked you in class when you blatantly ignored my attempts to get your red-headed attention." He brushed a strand of it away from my face. I had not done that. He had to be kidding. Wasn't he? "You're really smart. And I like that you say what you think and you don't giggle. You straight out laugh. I like that you asked us if no one was assaulted in our house or just not reported. That was a straight up balls to the wall question. I like you. I think you could like me, too."

I was sure I could. I didn't have that many friends, but I could tell Chance, Maven, and Banyan were good people. "If you're sure."

In my mind, my bank account stood up and cheered. Chance gave me a million dollar smile. "Awesome."

"Do you maybe want to check with Maven and Banyan? They might not want me there."

He walked back to my bookshelf. "They're good."

"How do you know that?" He couldn't just assume. Maven had given up his bed for me and run out first thing in the morning to check on the dorm fire. I wouldn't blame him if he was capital D-O-N-E, done with me.

Chance pointed at the books. "Pack some of these. I haven't read a whole bunch of them. I have to read non-school things to go to sleep at night. Looks like you're the same. I'll trade you some."

He liked fiction? My heart turned over right then. Maybe I had actually met someone who wanted to talk about non-literary books with me. Oh, I loved a classic, too. I was an English major, but yes, I loved mystery and romance and fantasy.

I kept my cool. "Okay."

If I was doing this, I had to get clothes and get moving on it.

"As to your question about how I know they won't mind? First, you'll be sleeping in my room, not theirs, and second, Maven chased you onto the street to learn your name and Banyan gave you his favorite sweatshirt. If I told them I let you go to a hotel, they'd simply drive to the hotel and get you themselves."

It had taken him a little bit to answer me, but I liked that one. They really wanted me around after just meeting me?

He wasn't done. "I'm feeding you before we go back. You haven't eaten yet, and I'm starving."

I looked over my shoulder. "I'd kill for some coffee."

"I know the perfect place, and it's open on Christmas."

I loved that idea.

FOUR

I stared down at the pancakes I'd managed to eat a quarter of before I was full. Could I take another bite? No, I absolutely could not. I rubbed my stomach. That had tasted amazing, but I couldn't fit another morsel in my stomach. Not without pain.

"How did you know this place was open on Christmas?" I hadn't even known it existed. I didn't have a car so I was stuck going to the places within walking distance of campus. Five miles was too far for me to go in search of food. I'd given myself a two mile radius as my stomping grounds.

He smiled as he swallowed his bacon. "I saw a sign they had up saying they'd be open."

The restaurant was full. We were clearly not the only two people who'd gone in search of sustenance on Christmas morning. "This is fantastic."

"I agree. I come here hungover most of the time. I knew I liked it, but boy do I like it more not hungover." He shook his head. "And that made me sound like a full on asshole."

I laughed. "No, it made you sound like a college guy."

"Maybe the same thing, right?" He winked at me. "What are you studying?"

There it was: the requisite *what's your major* question. "I'm an English major. How about you?"

"Biology and pre-med."

Now that was impressive. Our little college had a huge acceptance rate into medical school. All graduate schools, really. But med school acceptance was one of the ways the college sold itself to students. In the day of competition, as my father liked to say, all small liberal arts universities had to have something about them that made people want to go there as opposed to paying less at public universities and saving their money for graduate school.

Ours was theater and science. I wasn't in either program, but the head of the English department was world-renowned and I loved his classes.

"That's incredible." The brains of some of my class-mates never ceased to amaze me. I hated biology. I'd taken what basically amounted to *biology for people who are not good at it* as my requirement.

He waved his hand. "I don't know if it's incredible. It's what I always wanted to do. I'm good at science. I hated my English class. I had no idea what Shakespeare was saying. Just tell me what he's saying."

His green eyes sparkled when he talked. They were amazing to look at. "Are you from a family of doctors?"

"No, in fact. My family makes lingerie. Well, all kinds of women's clothing but mostly lingerie. Well, we don't physically make them. We are in the manufacturing of women's garments." He took a sip of his coffee. "There I spit that out."

I took a sip of mine. It was sweet. Molly always asked

me if I wanted any coffee with my sugar. Still, this was the way I liked it. "Bras. Panties?"

He nodded. "Yep. I've been slightly obsessed with women's undergarments since childhood."

"Have you?" This conversation had just taken a turn I hadn't seen coming. I dropped my eyes to his lips. Chance had a little smirk I hadn't seen him use before. "Good obsession or bad obsession? Like you think it's hot to wear women's underwear or you want to burn them in a big pile of flames?"

Wow. Yes. I had said that. It must have been the smirk. I wanted him to know I wasn't just some innocent flower. He couldn't say the words that were behind the lift of his mouth without recompense.

Chance leaned forward. "Awesome that you just said that. I fucking love that you just said that. I don't wear women's panties or bras. I like to see women in them. I'd like to see you in them. There I just said *that*. When you shut me in the hall to change your clothes before we left, I spent the whole time trying to picture which bras and panties you had. Does that bother you?"

I shook my head. "No. I like that a lot. I notice you haven't responded to the burning question?"

His smile broadened. "Why would I want to burn what I so like seeing intact?"

"Hey, Chance, just because we're talking like this doesn't mean I'm going to sleep with you tonight. Even if I want to."

He raised his eyebrows ever so slowly. "I didn't think it did. But I like that you want to. I've wanted to since you ignored me in class. That being said, I like this. This back and forth. I never get to do this." He shifted in his seat. "I'm hard as a rock right now. I can't move for a minute." He shook his head. "Fuck it."

Chance leaned over the table and kissed me, hard. Across the restaurant someone whistled and someone else clapped. I smiled against his mouth. He tasted like the strawberries from his waffles. And coffee. Yes, Chance could be addictive.

Finally, he pulled back and the waitress came over and set down our check. I looked down at my food. That was a side of me I tried really hard to keep to myself. I didn't say sexually provoking things in restaurants.

I had kissed his fraternity brother, a guy he spent holidays with on a boat, the night before. That wasn't okay. I couldn't just go around kissing them all because I wanted them. Could I?

No, that wasn't done. And I was sure the fraternity had some sort of code, a bros before hoes—much as I hated that word, I was pretty sure that was the expression—kind of a thing.

"Giovanna, don't get shy on me now. We'll just keep this between us. Just when we're alone. Okay? And just when we're both in the mood. You can say whatever you think quietly in your head. The stuff you don't say aloud usually, and I will stop being the perfectly polite gentleman I was raised to be and be this guy instead. I am that guy. But I also want to admit that pink panties are super hot and not be judged for it."

I raised my eyes. "I'd never judge you. I... think it's seriously hot."

"We have to stop, or I'm never getting out of this seat." He took a long drink from his water.

I reached for the check, and he grabbed it before I

could. "Please, let me buy you breakfast. It's really the least I could do."

"Stop. You'll never pay for anything when you're with me. I'm loaded. I hope the fact is the least interesting thing about me. I want to earn my own money, not live off the trust. Right now, I have it, I'm using it. I'm buying your breakfast."

I could keep arguing but that seemed fruitless. I supposed if he wanted to buy my breakfast, that was fine.

He got out of the seat, slightly adjusting his pants when he did. "Come on. I'm actually exhausted. Time to conk out for a few hours. Oh, Giovanna, I'm still safe, okay? I'd never do anything that wasn't consensual. I like you."

I took his hand while he paid the cashier. "I didn't ignore you in class. I mean, not just you. I don't look at anyone if I can help it. I know what I just did here might negate this, but the truth is I'm shy."

"Well, if that's true then I'll take it as a compliment that you open up around me. And I'll let it go that you didn't smile back the hundred times I smiled at you."

How could I have missed that? A guy this good looking had been smiling at me, and I'd missed the whole thing?

Well, I was glad I'd gotten a chance to spend the morning with him. Talking about underwear. I smiled. What a strange Christmas this proved to be.

When we got back to SPiI, it was quiet. The kind of stillness when people were sleeping. "The pledges are finishing up, and then they'll go home. I think Maven is probably out cold, and who knows with Banyan, but I don't hear his music so he's probably asleep, too. Sorry to ditch you on Christmas. I can stay up for a bit if you want."

I shook my head. "Don't be silly. I can sit in there at one of the tables and work on the literary magazine. That's what

I was going to do today anyway. And read. Did you guys have dinner plans? I could cook us something."

"We didn't get as far as eating in our thoughts. Last Christmas, we fished. Badly. But we caught a few things. So sure, if you want to cook, that would be great." He grinned. "I loved today. You're not freaked out with me, right?"

I stopped for a second to consider his question. "No, actually. I'm maybe less freaked out. I don't know what to do when people seem too inherently nice. In my heart, I believe most people, especially me, have a side they rarely show the world. Sometimes it's dark. Sometimes it's just different, or unconventional. But it's there. I think maybe we showed each other a touch of that side."

"I like it." He bent over, pressing his lips to mine gently. "If you want a nap, my room is the one right next to Maven's on the left if you're facing the rooms at the top of the stairs. To get to Banyan's, should you need, head to the very top of the house. He has the loft in the attic."

I almost told him what color underwear I had on. But that would have been too much, for now. "Chance, my friends call me Vonni." Or at least they did when I was younger because they'd hear my parents do it.

He leaned against the railing of the stairs. "Vonni. It suits you."

I loved that he thought so.

I LOVED RUNNING the literary magazine, but I wasn't always sure I was the right person for the job. I had a hard time telling what was good and what really wasn't. If I didn't like something, was that just a voice problem? Did I not enjoy the way the author told the story and so therefore no one would? There had to be a line somewhere that I didn't cross. Some things had to be rejected. But that was such a problem with art. There were good stories that just needed work.

We had editors. How could I tell what was fixable and what really wasn't?

I sighed. I'd rejected an entry for this month's magazine, and I'd do it again. But I was liking the mystery serial that had been sent to me, sort of. I was going to put it in the decidedly maybe pile.

I'd spent Christmas almost entirely the same way the year before, only now I was doing it in a frat house.

That reminded me that I had unread messages from Molly.

I grabbed my phone and skimmed through them.

He didn't show up. How could he do that? The whole family was expecting to meet him.

I groaned. R.J. was a good boyfriend to Molly except when he wasn't, and then he was downright awful. Ditching Christmas? Yes, that was very bad. But bad enough for my roommate to want to be done with him? Probably not. Molly, as far as I could tell, liked the excitement being with R.J. brought to her life. She didn't want to be Greek herself but she didn't mind reaping whatever benefits girlfriends had by being with him.

I'm so sorry. Did he explain?

It took a moment but then she answered. *Oh thank goodness. I was so worried. I just got the email. You're okay?*

I nodded and then laughed. She couldn't see it. Sometimes I was such a dork. *Yep. Scary but fine. Our room is fine, too. What happened with R.J.?*

He said he took some cold meds, and it knocked him out. He's here now. My family is fine with it so I guess I am, too.

You're okay? Where are you staying? Do you need to come here?

I knew what it was like to take cold medicine and be out for the count. Allergy meds and cold medicine tended to put me on my rear for twelve hours. My mother was the same way.

I'm okay. You'll never believe this, but I'm actually staying at the SPiI house. I was going to be as brief about this as I could be. *They saw me in need, and they let me temporarily move in. Most of them aren't here.*

It wasn't that I didn't want to talk to Molly about it, but there were certain details I didn't want to be pressed on. Like the fact that I'd kissed two of them. What was I doing? I couldn't go around kissing two fraternity brothers who seemed like good friends. I didn't go around kissing everyone I met. I rubbed my eyes.

What? !!! Which SPiI brothers? That is just so...not you.

She was right. It really wasn't me. I ignored the question. *What are you and R.J. going to be doing now?*

It seemed two could play at that game. She didn't respond to me either. She finished her own thought. *R.J. says to be careful with the SPiI brothers. They're very intense and not all that nice. He hates them all with a passion.*

Well, R.J. could kiss my ass. I rolled my eyes. I hated him. I really did. I was trying to be a good friend because he, mostly, made my friend happy, but his not liking them meant that I would like them even more. The only thing he and I could agree on was that Molly was awesome.

Thank you. That was about all I could answer.

I miss you. She replied. *Do yourself a favor and when you have a minute, check out greeklifeoncampus.com. Download the app and look up our school. Whoever you're hanging out with will have a posting in there. Every member of the Greek circle does. Even R.J. Sometimes it's harsh, but it's almost never a lie. Hugs. Love you. Be safe.*

I sighed. I wasn't going to go into an app to read about Maven, Chance, and Banyan. They made an app for that? No, that felt like reading gossip pages on the internet. I went back to reading the entry. Who was I kidding? The writing was terrible. Rejection. I hated to do it but that was my role. Feeling sick about it in my stomach, I sat down to read my book for a bit.

I was halfway through my book when Banyan stumbled into the room. I'd only been back a few hours. That couldn't be enough sleep for him, could it?

He half tripped, half walked over to the couch where I sat. "Hey, Giovanna."

"Hi, Banyan." I touched his back. "You okay?"

"Yep. I have bad dreams. It'll pass."

We were in the back of the main room with the chairs and tables. I'd discovered that farther in the room were couches and fireplaces. I certainly knew what nightmares were like. I rubbed his back slowly, using a circular, unchanging motion. He rubbed at his eyes, eventually lifting his head to grin at me. "Thank you for the rub. It helped bring me back here and away from the bodiless heads floating at me."

Well, that would be disturbing. "I'm glad."

"Me, too." He stretched his arms over his head. "Merry Christmas. Again. Glad you're here."

I guessed it would be up to me to tell him. "Chance invited me to stay. I can go if it's a problem."

"Where would you go?" He cocked his head to the side.

"A hotel. I was halfway through booking it when he stopped me."

Banyan scrunched up his whole face. "Oh, not the hotel

here. No. If you want to go to a hotel, we'll go somewhere cool. Pick a place. We'll go to a hotel there."

I smiled. "Very funny."

"Who's joking? Pick a place; we will go right now."

I adjusted where I sat to stare at him. "You're serious."

"Almost always. Even when I'm joking."

Well, that would be a good thing to remember about him. "I can't go somewhere. The hotel here in the middle of Pennsylvania would stretch my budget."

"Okay, I'll pay. I was going to anyway." He waited for a second like he wanted me to respond, and when I didn't, he spoke again. "Pick a place. Anywhere in the world."

I sighed. "Banyan, we just met. I can't go away with you and have you pay. Those are actually two separate clauses. I can't go away with you because we just met. And I can't have you pay because we just met. It's bad enough Chance insisted on paying for breakfast."

He sat up straight. "Chance can take you for food, but I can't take you away? How is that okay?"

"They're not nearly the same thing and..." I stopped. "You're screwing with me. From moment one. Okay, ha ha. I've been had."

He sank down into the couch and leaned on the arm. "I'm not, actually. There's not much of a difference for me."

I'd never felt poor in my life until I'd come to this school. It tended to have an extremely wealthy student body. I knew what real poverty was. I'd seen it. Stood near people who would kill for the ten dollars an hour Molly complained about getting for babysitting her sister. Everyone else got fifteen. Everyone she knew, anyway. I was privileged, but the kids here were something else. They were downright scary wealthy.

As an only child, my parents were able to do things for

me that they'd never have been able to do if I'd had siblings. Tuition, for example. But, for most of the students here, they never had to think about it at all.

Their parents didn't either.

"Banyan, even with whatever your budget is, a trip is not the same as pancakes." He'd talked me through circles in this conversation. Did he do this with everyone or was this somehow reserved for me on Christmas Day?

"I don't have a budget." He yawned. "Hate me yet?"

I didn't follow his question. "Why would I hate you?"

"I think you mean that. Okay, so you won't go away with me because we just met." He lifted his eyebrows. "We have to leave the money out of it because I don't think we'll ever see eye to eye on that subject. I take people away with me all of the time that I've just met and I pay for them. Well, maybe not all the time. Once a quarter? Fine. You don't like that idea. Where would you go with me if you knew me better?"

I sighed. "If I answer that question, are you going to order a plane? I'm not going to answer if you are intending to do so, nor will I get on the plane even if it suddenly arrives with a full crew intending to fly off into the deep blue yonder."

"I love how you talk. Okay, no ordering planes. This is purely hypothetical, and for some kind of future knowledge, maybe."

I thought about it. His question was actually an interesting one. "Where would you go?"

"You tell me first."

The problem was I didn't have an easy answer. "I've been all over the world. I'm really lucky that way. Places most people won't ever see. I'll be spending my summer in India." Assuming my parents were still alive and not poison darted to death. I really had to stop thinking about that.

"So no India. Got it." He had a lazy look on his face, as though he was purely content to continue waiting for me until whenever it was I came up with an answer.

"Oh!" I nodded, smiling as the answer came to me. "I've never been to the Grand Canyon. I'd like to go to the Grand Canyon."

The pure joy in his grin surprised me. "I've never been either."

"Really? I would have thought you'd been everywhere you wanted to go."

Banyan ran a hand through his light brown hair. "I've never thought about going. It's a thing people do with their parents, right? My dad is only in the picture occasionally, and I cannot imagine my mom in her stiletto heels wandering around the Grand Canyon. So, no. We'll do it, okay? When you know me better. We'll go."

"Maybe. If I can figure out how to pay for myself to go." He groaned, and I held up a finger to stop him. "Banyan, I don't care if you could pay for the whole world to go to the Grand Canyon. I'm never going to want you to pay for me. I'd feel... like I was taking advantage of you. We'll go. When I can pay for it. So you know I wanted to go just to be there with you and not because I wanted something from you."

He leaned forward and pinched my arm. I yelped. It stung. "What in the hell?"

"I'm trying to make sure you're real."

I stood up. "I'm real, and I'm a redhead, so I am going to have a big ugly bruise from that, thank you very much."

"Do you want to play video games? I can't get my painting right. I fell asleep, had a nightmare, and now I'm off kilter."

I shook my head. "Sounds like fun, but I promised Chance I'd cook. I should get started with that. I'm not even sure what food you have here, so this might be challenging."

He got to his feet. "I'd offer to help, but I've literally never made anything but a sandwich in the kitchen. Our pledge master didn't have us baking like Chance does with these guys. He's much more interested in food than the brother we had. Ours was much more interested in drinks. I make a killer cocktail."

"Well, I could show you. Basic stuff if you want. But only if you want to. No pressure." I pointed toward the kitchen. "That's where I'll be."

He didn't hesitate, following after me quickly. "I'd love it. If I get in the way just tell me to leave."

"Banyan." I said his name, and it dawned on me what I should have noticed earlier. "That's like the name of the library. Banyan Library. Were you named after it?"

He shook his head walking to the fridge. "I shouldn't say no. It's complicated. Banyan is my father's last name. He knocked up my mother. Not his wife. His wife didn't much care for that so... I'm the worst kept secret in the world. He couldn't claim me but he pays for me. Mom gave me his last name as my first name; sort of as a fuck you to him. She thought he'd leave his wife and marry her. Not very smart my mother. Most people just think I'm named after a tree, but if you ever met my mom, you'd know she doesn't know one tree from another. I let them think that. Looks like Maven bought a turkey. He does things like that. Thinks about what we'd need to eat."

I nodded. It was a good thing I really wasn't impressed with how much money people had—or that I didn't care if they had any at all. Otherwise, I might have suddenly been overwhelmed that Banyan was probably from the Banyan

Oil and Gas family. About every third time I filled my father's car, I used that station.

Rolling up the sleeves of the black, cotton, paint-stained sweatshirt he'd given me, I had to wonder who this man was. The artist whose work I commissioned for the literary magazine because it was brilliant, or the easygoing rich guy who wanted to fly wherever tonight? I supposed, like all of us, he was complicated, and probably both.

FIVE

Maven had bought turkey, and it turned out to be pre-cooked so all I had to do was warm it up. He hadn't thought about side dishes, so I made do. They had a lot of soup in the house. Did everyone eat french onion soup in the SPiI house?

I set Banyan chopping vegetables that were in a second fridge in the back. He hummed while he worked. I listened to the friendly sound. I stirred the soup and tried to think of anything else I could invent for Christmas Dinner out of what they had. It dawned on me fast: I could bake brownies. Not great for the main meal but perfect for dessert.

They had everything I needed. I used to bake all the time when I was in high school. It had become sort of a hobby until my mom thought she was gaining weight. I'd had to stop then because she refused to let the ingredients into the house.

"You couldn't have taken me away." I had to say something because all I could think about was how sexy he would look in the kitchen shirtless. Maybe I needed to go to the doctor and tell them I was obsessed with sex. Maybe there was a pill. "You, ah, have to do community service."

He nodded. "True. That is true. What happened is mostly my fault anyway."

"I don't understand. Isn't Chance in charge of the pledges?" The ins and outs of how their fraternity worked eluded me. Probably because I stayed away from the frat houses. And now I was trying to understand them all at once.

"He does, indeed. But it was me who told them about how we hoisted underwear up the Dean's flagpole when we were pledges. They wanted to repeat what we did. That's on me."

I stopped stirring. "You did? What happened to Maven's whole take on responsibility and not being stupid for the frat?"

"That's why we pledge. To stop being asshats who hoist underwear and become people who don't. I think their repeating it was meant to be sort of a... thank you to the seniors. Like hey, we acknowledge you guys and think you're awesome." He shook his head. "Chance took all the heat. He's in charge. And Maven threatened to step down if the frat board didn't back off of Chance. But it's really all my fault. Ouch." Banyan dropped his knife. "Damn it. Sorry. I'm useless. I should have remembered that."

He was bleeding, just a little bit. I grabbed his hand and put it under some running water. "Stop that. You are not useless. You cut yourself. It happens. To all of us. Me all the time. I'm clumsy." I hated how he said he was useless; the tone of his voice, it was full of disdain for himself. I dried off his finger with a paper towel.

"Band-Aid?" I had no idea where they'd be.

"I'll get them. I can do it. Thank you, though." He

crossed past me out of the room and returned in a second with his finger bandaged.

I wanted to curl up in a ball and just rock back and forth. Why had I grabbed his hand and offered to bandage him like he was a baby? Of course he could take care of his own dang finger. I closed my eyes. One. Two. Three. Four. Five. I counted to five whenever I made a fool of myself to re-center and remind myself why I preferred to be left alone most of the time.

"You okay?" Banyan stood in front of me when I opened my eyes. "What's wrong?"

There wasn't going to be getting out of this. Not without addressing what I'd done. "Banyan, I had no business grabbing your hand and treating you like you didn't know how to take care of your own wound."

"Giovanna." He ran his non-bandaged hand through my hair. "Do you think I'm upset? No one has given two fucks if I cut myself since my mother fired the nanny when I was ten and told me to take care of myself. Oh, those two sleeping upstairs would care if I had a big gaping wound. Otherwise, it's just me. It was super sweet."

His mouth pressed to mine. I closed my eyes and let him kiss me. For a second, I just enjoyed the sensation of his sweet lips touching my own, but then I kissed him back. He tugged me tighter to him, and I wrapped my arms around his neck to hold on. He was much taller than I was, and I had to go up on tiptoes to reach him.

Banyan smiled against my lips before he hoisted me onto the counter. "Smart thinking," I whispered.

"I can be adept when I want to kiss the prettiest girl I've seen in years."

I raised my eyebrows. It didn't feel weird talking this close together, although I was sure it would if we tried it in the future. Sometimes things only worked the very moment I did them and never again. After, they got weird. "You're a charmer, Banyan. I'll give you that."

"Not usually, no."

The timer for my brownies dinged, and I gasped. I had to get them out. "Sorry. I've got to get down."

"Boo. Okay, fine. I'll get back to the veggies."

I jumped down off the counter.

It was when I pulled the brownies out of the oven that it dawned on me I'd kissed all three SPiI brothers that were here within twenty-four hours. I closed my eyes. I couldn't do that. Not with all three of them. It wasn't right. It wasn't honest.

The problem was that I had no idea which one of them I would pick to kiss if I was forced to. And the more likely scenario was I'd pissed them all off, they'd kick me out, and that would be that.

What was the matter with me?

"Hey." Maven walked into the room barefoot. "I smelled food. Did you cook?"

"She did," Banyan answered. "I'm helping, badly, but it's really all her."

I placed the brownies on the counter. "Least I could do. Chance said I could stay. Is that okay?"

Maven looked soft from having been asleep. His eyes were slightly hooded. "Sure. Love it. My bed smelled like you. Roses, I think. Good scent. Sorry, rambling. Yes, stay. You don't have to cook to do so either."

"I won't take your bed again. Chance said there were two beds in his room."

Banyan shook his head. "Screw that. You can sleep in my room. It's bigger. I also have two beds. You'll like my room better. You won't have to look at every sports hero Chance loves in the world displayed around the room."

"It wasn't a problem," Maven interrupted Banyan. "I can even drag a second bed into my room if you want."

Well, finding a place to sleep wasn't going to be a problem. But figuring out what to do next was.

Chance woke up a few minutes later and came downstairs, which meant it was time to eat soon. I warmed the turkey and we sat down around one of the tables.

"I would have warmed the turkey, Giovanna, but I wouldn't have made vegetables or brownies. So thank you. Oh, and for the soup." He made eye contact with Chance and Banyan. "I haven't eaten this stuff in years."

None of them were touching their soup. "Can I ask what the deal with the soup is?"

"You can, but we can't tell you." Chance dug into the turkey. "I'm sorry. Some things are secret."

They'd told me that before. "I get it."

Although I might never fully understand the intricacies of this stuff, I did understand secrets. There were things I would never tell people about my life unless I really trusted them. The way my mother would start crying a lot at night and the next thing I knew, one of them would accept a new grant and we'd all leave Boston again. She wasn't okay unless they were somewhere other than home.

I pushed that memory away. Maven rose from the table and returned with four beers. He offered me one, which I declined.

Chance took a long drink from his. "So do you not drink because you just don't, or maybe you're a recovering alcoholic, or you hate the taste, or you're counting calories?"

"Are those my only choices?" I liked teasing Chance because he liked it.

He grinned. "No. Not if it's not one of those answers."

"Don't grill the girl." Banyan opened his bottle. "I like her. I don't want her to leave because you're suddenly twenty questions. Maybe she doesn't drink because she doesn't drink."

I don't drink because when my father does, he gets sad and I don't want to risk being that way. "I just don't. Many reasons I guess, but mostly, I just don't."

Maven got to his feet again. He didn't seem to sit still very long. "I'm going to make a fire. Dean Brown can kiss my ass if he doesn't like it. Giovanna, we're technically not supposed to use our fireplace. But I bet he's drunk on eggnog and won't notice tonight. If he comes over, I'll pay the fine personally. Unless, it's too soon? Sorry, not thinking you've just been through an ordeal. I thought brownies by fireplace."

"I like that idea. I guess I won't know if it's too soon until I give it a try."

Maven held out his hand for me. "Fair enough."

That had been the quickest consumption of food ever. I think we'd been at the table five minutes. I took Maven's hand and let him lead me from the living room.

"What gets me about this is the fact that you know how to light a fire, Mave." Banyan was right behind us. "Since when?"

"I used to get sent to sleepaway camp over the summer. They taught us things. I had the idea that it might be cool to light one when everyone was away, and I bought the stuff last week."

Chance joined us, handing me a water as he entered the living room. I stood, flanked by Chance and Banyan as we all stared at Maven making the fire. He wasn't actually all that adept at it. I could make a fire in a fireplace a lot faster than he was doing it, but I wasn't going to interfere. This had been his idea. He'd figure it out, and if he didn't, I'd help him when he was done.

Instead, I let Chance lead me to the couch. There was a flat screen television above the fireplace. Banyan turned it on from some app on his phone, and a football game appeared. He sat down next to me, and Chance took the other side. There was room for Maven next to him. Banyan elbowed me gently. "Merry Christmas, Giovanna."

"Thank you. Merry Christmas, Banyan."

Maven got the fire lit and flopped down on the couch in the space for him. A pitter-patter started on the roof, and I groaned. This time of year that wasn't just rain, it was freezing rain. Chance yawned. "Tell me again why we all went to college here instead of, say, Miami?"

"I liked the chair of the English department." It was only after I answered that I realized he'd basically been making a joke. I really needed to get out more.

Banyan stretched out his legs onto the coffee table. "My father gave so much money to this place he has his last name on the library. They kind of had to take me. I got into a lot of shit my senior year. I was all but kicked out of my school. I'm perfectly smart grades wise. But this was kind of my only choice. The old man said this was where I was going. So here I am."

"What did you do?"

His eyes were far away. "One of my half-brothers went to the high school, too. He started some shit. I ended it."

"Don't leave it like that; she's going to think you killed him." Maven groaned. "They were in the same boarding school. Holden called Banyan's mother a slut. Banyan spray painted the word douchebag on his car."

That actually didn't sound as bad as I'd imagined. Me

and my imagination... I'd been picturing drugs or explosions. "Seems like you were pretty tame."

"They have a zero tolerance policy for fucking up. They didn't give a shit what he'd said. I was banned from leaving my room. Went to class, back to my room. Six months. And they marked up my permanent record as being problematic. I don't know what would have happened if I'd applied other places. By that point, my ability to resist was gone. I just wanted peace and to be away from the last-named Banyans."

I touched his arm. "I'm sorry."

"I'm not. Got me here. Met these two and the rest of my pledge brothers. Found art. Sitting here. All is well."

"Since we're playing this game"—Maven laughed—"I'm here because it's not in New York. I needed to get out of the city where everyone knew my father was a felon. My uncle suggested I apply here. I did. I got in. It's a good school. Some people know the deal here, but I'm not faced with it daily."

Chance yawned again. "Your old man has nothing to do with you."

"Thanks. You know that and I know that, but you'd think I'd committed the crime from how my classmates acted. They threw me off student council."

This was so interesting. Sitting here with all of them, listening to them tell their stories, hearing how they talked to each other. They were comfortable. On their own, individually, they could come across intimidating but not like this.

I liked this. A lot.

Chance sighed. "High admittance into medical school. I'm not going straight in. A lot of people take a few years and do medical research now before. But when

I do apply, I want my undergraduate to have been from here."

And here we all were. Maven pointed at the television. "That's holding. No, that's not cool. Throw the flag."

I guessed they were watching the television, too. I'd never followed football, and so I let my gaze fall to where the fire burned. It didn't bother me at all. This was different than the scary smoke filled hallways that I'd run from. I wasn't alone, and the fire was contained.

Banyan and Maven occasionally said something about the game, but Chance was so quiet I stole a look at him. His eyes were closed. He was asleep, beer still in his hand. When I took it from him, he didn't stir.

I'd set it on the table before Maven spoke. "He has way too much on his plate and that's Banyan's and my fault. We talked him into taking on pledge master. There's no one better, but he has to keep his GPA astronomically high. It's a lot all the time. My applications to law school are at least already in. I'm just waiting."

We stayed silent after that, my guilt starting to eat at me. I had kissed all of them, and they weren't these sort of distantly good looking yet interesting guys anymore. They were real people with history and dreams. They were very close friends. I couldn't be this girl who came in and screwed with their lives.

Chance never stirred, not even a little, and when the game was finally over, Maven shook his shoulder gently. "Come on, man, up to your bed. You'll get a sore neck if you sleep like that, and we have to clean the garden area of campus tomorrow."

"Fuck." Chance rubbed at his eyes. "I didn't mean to fall asleep."

"Yeah, well, you snored so loud poor Giovanna lost

some of her hearing." Banyan reached over me and shoved at Chance's shoulder.

Chance turned to me. "Sorry. I don't think I usually snore."

"You didn't. He's teasing you."

Next to me, he groaned. "I'm too out of it to catch that shit right now. Going to come up with me, Vonni, or are you up for a while?"

"Why shorten Giovanna when it's so sexy as it is?" Banyan set down his drink.

The things he said would go to my head if I didn't see how easily they left his mouth. Some guys were flirts.

"Because her friends call her Vonni, and I want to."

It was now or never. I had to tell the truth. There was nothing else for it. "Guys, I think I should leave. Hopefully the hotel has a room. Listen, before you argue, I did something kind of shitty today. Over the last twenty-four hours, I kissed all three of you. This is very unlike me. I haven't kissed anyone in almost three and a half years." I wouldn't sugarcoat it. "I know that's really bad. You guys are really close, and I'm not going to make it weird. So I'll go."

I rose but Banyan grabbed my arm and pulled me back down. "Hold up. Don't go anywhere. I kissed you. Sure you kissed me back, but I initiated."

"Same." Maven turned off the television.

Chance looked more alert than he had been a minute earlier. "For sure on me, too."

"So." Maven nodded. "You didn't technically kiss any of us."

They really didn't look mad. "Are you three sort of storing your anger to what happened inside, or do you really not care?"

"Lots of girls kiss all of us." Banyan uttered the statement so simply I might have thought it was no big deal at all except that it was... weird.

Maven rose. "Lots of girls who aren't exactly like Giovanna. There is a certain girl here on campus who really just wants to hook up with frat guys. Some of them pick a house. It's always consensual. But they come, and they don't much care which one of us they're hooking up with. Sometimes we're not all that interested in who it is either."

"I..." I shook my head. "I'm not sure what even to make of that."

"Yes, I know, because you're the kind of girl who thinks we would kick you out Christmas night for kissing us." He pointed to Chance and Banyan. "You like all of us? Like you'd like to kiss all of us."

I swallowed. "Yes."

Maven made eye contact with Banyan and Chance. "That's fine. We'll just keep it light. Friends who kiss. It doesn't have to be a big deal. You're not looking for a boyfriend right, Giovanna? I have to tell you that the three of us are not that. We're pretty much terrible boyfriends. We could give you references of women who could attest to that."

I rose, and Banyan let me. "No, I don't want a boyfriend. I wasn't good in a relationship either. I could never come up with enough conversation. And I don't have the time because I actually have to study all the time. I don't have the time to worry about someone else's schedule or needs. I kind of have to be selfish until I graduate."

"Awesome. Feel free to keep kissing all of us, Vonni." Chance ran a hand through his hair. "We'll keep it light. That works for us. And when it's over, we can all be friends. That really goes the best. No expectations. No hold on each other."

"How far does this go?" I really couldn't believe this was happening. "I have to tell you"—I took a really deep breath. I shouldn't feel shame about this but sometimes I did. I didn't want to analyze why, not right then anyway—"I really like sex. When things get hot and heavy, I'm not going to want to hold off. Could we all have sex?"

Banyan choked on his beer. In between coughs, he spoke. "Sorry, didn't see that coming. Sure, baby, if you want to have sex, we're game. But it's all about you. Love is love, but we're not into each other that way. Fine for anyone who is."

I shook my head. "I didn't mean you guys. I meant with me."

I wouldn't tell them right then about my ménage fantasies. I had books for that. My body buzzed. Could this be real?

"Not one of us is going to say no to that, but that's up to you. Always about the girl's choice with me. Again, as long as no feelings get hurt on your end, we'll be golden." Chance yawned. "Going to bed. Come up when you're ready. I'll be out cold. No sex from me tonight." He winked. "I'd be nothing but a disappointment."

Maven stopped him with his words. "One more thing. Giovanna's not interested in building a rep, I don't think, by sleeping with SPiI brothers. Are you, Giovanna?"

I swallowed. "Not even a little bit. I mean I have nothing against SPiI brothers, but the administration knows my parents. Things start getting around to the point that they hear it, repeat it, and I'm going to have to deal with discomfort I'd rather not face."

"Then we keep this just amongst the four of us. Deal? When it's over it's over, but no one ever knows she was anything more than our regular platonic friend. We're leaving in May. She has to stay here another year and a half."

Chance nodded. "Deal."

Banyan took my hand and kissed it. "Deal. And no more talking about leaving unless we piss you off. Even then, you tell us first, okay? I just met you, but I like you here."

"Okay, then, I'll stay."

We'd just agreed to keep it light, and I could have sex with all of them if I wanted to. For the rest of my life, I would know this happened. When I was old and living with my cats—à la the tragic novel of my life I occasionally wrote in my head—talking to myself, I would remember that this happened. Three of the hottest guys I'd ever seen wanted me to stay for two weeks and were interested in me sexually.

"I guess I'll go to bed, too. Merry Christmas." I'd left my suitcase in the hallway. I retrieved it. Chance waited at the bottom of the stairs for me, where he took my bag.

There were fourteen days until school started. I meant to make the most of them. In all of the ways possible.

SIX

Chance's room wasn't nearly the shrine to sports that Banyan had made it out to be. He had a few posters on the walls, mostly from the Yankees, and some signed pictures he had of football players. I didn't know which team.

He'd gone to use the bathroom, and I was going to use it when he was done. I needed a shower. How did the girls who slept here all the time deal with this? What did Molly do at DKI? Did she rush back to the dorm to shower, and I just never knew?

My life had shifted so suddenly in twenty-four hours. I'd never, in a million years, worried about this. Greek life was for other people, not me.

Chance came through the door. He was in a pair of black boxer shorts and a gray t-shirt that clung to all of his muscles. I tried not to stare, which involved me looking everywhere but at him.

He crossed past me. "You should take the bed on the right."

Chance's room was set up differently than Maven's. He had two beds. One bigger, a full size, and a twin in the corner. His chest of drawers was in his closet, taking up all the space except for the storage about the cabinet and his hanging clothes were in a moveable closet in the remaining corner of the room. He had a small desk right next to the bed. He was right when he said he had his own organization system. There were piles everywhere.

"You take the bed on the right."

I looked where he pointed. "No way. That's the bigger one. I'm much smaller than you. You don't sleep in the twin, you sleep in the full." Just general deduction could show me that. "I bet at home you have a king size to be comfortable. No way am I sticking you out of your own bed. I'm good in a twin."

He rubbed his eyes. "You're not going to give on this, are you?"

"No." I could be stubborn when I wanted to be. This was ridiculous. I wasn't going to let him be uncomfortable.

"Okay, I'll take the big one."

"Great." I rocked back on my feet. "I'm going to go shower, and I'll come right back."

"Sounds good. You know I'm usually really energetic. I think a lot of things are just catching up all at once." He pointed to his desk. "Top left, I have a pile of books. I think you'll like a couple of them. Where are yours? I'm borrowing them. This is me sort of asking sort of telling you that I'm salivating for the books."

I grinned at him. He was seriously cute. "Top of the suitcase. Take whichever ones you want. I'll look at yours when I come back in."

"You're so cool. You don't make things hard. Speak your mind. Even when it's difficult. That conversation downstairs should have taken five shots of tequila. You did that stone cold sober. That was balls to the wall and, as it is, we all get what we want, right? You're different than I thought you would be."

I wasn't surprised. "I don't... talk about how I think about sex all the time. Anyway, enough of this."

He leaned against the desk. "Go shower. We'll talk after I pick out which of your books I'm stealing."

I grabbed my stuff from my second suitcase and traveled down the hall. Maven's room was quiet, but upstairs, I heard Banyan playing low music. I still had yet to see his room that they said he painted in. I needed to give him back his sweatshirt.

The shower had good spray, and it felt nice to get really clean. I brushed my teeth, towel dried my frizzy curls that I could only manage to control for brief periods of time, and headed back down to Chance's room. When this place was full, it must be loud all the time.

Everything was clean. Did they do it themselves or did someone come in? We had a cleaner at the dorm who did the hallways but not our personal rooms. Maybe it was the same here. And who did they pay to live here? The school? The overall Greek organization? Was that secret?

I opened Chance's door and walked in. The overhead ceiling fan making a slight whoosh was the only sound in the room. Chance was sprawled out in his bed, shoes still on, covers askew beneath him. My book, The Tale of Two Men, a gory thriller that had kept me up for weeks after I read it, lay on his chest. His eyes were closed. He'd fallen asleep fully clothed with the lights on.

I really hadn't taken that long.

He wouldn't be comfortable like that. I walked over to him and gently took off his shoes. Then I took the book off his chest and covered him with the blankets I could get loose from beneath him without disturbing him too much.

Chance mumbled something and then turned over, his back to me, his face toward the wall.

He'd feel better. I shut off the light. If I wanted to read, I'd do it by the light from my phone.

Molly had texted as well as my friends, Sharon and Alexis. I guess the word was out that I was staying at the SPiI house. Leave it to Molly to spread the word.

I was certainly not going to tell them the truth. This was between me and the three guys I'd just agreed to have an open, sleeping together but just friends relationship with.

Nothing really to report, ladies. Most of the brotherhood isn't here. Just a few, and they are generously letting me stay. Miss you all. If I have any stories, I'll share them.

I wouldn't. The next fourteen days were just for me.

I grabbed one of Chance's books that I hadn't read—it looked to be a murder mystery—and set out to read it. The prose was good, and it had my attention quickly. Two hours later, I forced myself to stop. I'd read all night and be a zombie the next day. With the way things were going, I had to be able to handle things changing very quickly.

I slept hard. It seemed like no time had passed when light traveled through the window to bring me back to real life. I rubbed my eyes. Across the room, Chance made a noise, and I forced my lids open to look at him.

"Hey." He lay on his side. "Sorry, I woke you. I woke myself up talking in my sleep. It's early. Go back to sleep."

I yawned. "I'm up." I looked at the clock on my phone. Five-thirty. He was right. It was too early. But the sun was up, so I'd be able to see the snow on the ground and not kill myself on the ice. "I'm going to see if I can manage a jog."

"No." He held out his hand. "You'll fall and break something. It's icy. Remember last night?"

The freezing rain. I'd all but forgotten. "You're right."

He wiggled his fingers. "Don't leave me hanging. Come and cuddle. I didn't get to talk to you last night because I'm acting like I'm one hundred years old. Come on."

I slipped out of bed before I could overthink it. What had seemed so easy last night with the fire and the brownies seemed a little bit more intimidating in the light of day. I'd never agreed to potentially have sex with three guys I barely knew before. The desire was still there, but my confidence was lagging.

Chance took my hand when I got close and drew me against him before he covered us in his blankets. "Did you take care of me last night? Take off my shoes? Cover me up?"

"I did."

He spooned behind me, his arm coming over my waist. "You're sweet. Thank you."

"You're welcome."

Chance kissed the spot where my shoulder met my neck. "Go back to sleep. We can doze like this. Don't tell anyone, but I like to cuddle. Or at least I think I do. I don't have that much experience with it. I like that you're here and it's not time for us to get up."

I closed my eyes. I'd worry about the decisions I'd made later. He was right. We could just do this for a while.

A SOUND down the hall roused me again. It took me a second to realize it was loud, punk music coming from upstairs. Not down the hall. I rubbed my eyes.

"Hey." Chance kissed me in the same spot as earlier. "Banyan is loud, but it's nothing compared to how loud some of the other guys are."

I rolled over slightly to look at him. He was rumpled. "Did you get any more sleep?"

"I did, but then I woke up because being this close to you got me hard."

We were cocooned in his room. I rolled over until I faced him completely. "Good morning, Chance."

"Good morning, Vonni. Did you sleep well in my room?" He placed his hand on top of my head, stroking my hair.

I nodded. "I did. Did you sleep okay with me in your room?"

"Really well."

Our lips met. I didn't know who kissed who first, but soon we were connected, mouth-to-mouth. Pressed as close as I was to him, I could feel just how hard he was. I reached between us, finding the slit of his boxer shorts. Was there anything sexier than a man aroused? If there was, I didn't know what it was. He'd gotten this way because he was turned on by *me*.

I clasped the top of his cock, and he moaned. Chance sighed against my mouth. "You don't have to."

"I want to." I really did.

I tugged his boxers down until they were down around his ankles. My hand found his hardness again, and I stroked him, from balls to his tip. His cock jumped in my hand. Chance grabbed the top of my pajama pants. "Take them off."

"You don't have to." I mimicked his words from earlier.

He shook his head. "I want to and..." He sucked in his breath at my ministrations. "It's so much better if I can get you off, too. It's so much more exciting. And it's already pretty damn exciting."

I squirmed out of my pants. I never wore underwear to bed. He pressed his finger inside of me. "You're wet for me."

His voice was low; it sent shivers through my body. "I'm so hot for you."

"Same."

Chance searched for a second for my clit. "Sorry, I'll find it. I'll..."

He did, and I moaned, closing my eyes. I stroked him, a long pull on his cock, and his hips bucked against me. He kissed me, lightly, and then all we did was breathe. Touch. Caress until I was throbbing with need, and he pulsed in my hand. Chance wasn't steady at first, but he found the rhythm I liked with a little encouragement, and then he was giving me the right kind of pressure, the exact touch I needed.

"Fuck," he whispered. "I'm close."

"So come." I wanted him to, so much.

"Not until you do." He pressed against me harder, pinching my bundle of nerves, and I exploded. I hadn't known I needed that or I would have asked for it, but he had been right on. I jerked against him, and he came in my hand. Chance kissed me hard, his tongue finding mine. We stayed like that, both of us shaking, wrapped in his blankets as the pleasure we'd just given each other moved through us slowly.

Eventually, he kissed my lips in a gentle caress. "Wow."

I smiled. "Morning."

His laugh was low. "Yep. Morning. Hold on." He got out of bed, pulling on his boxers. "I'm going to get you a wet towel."

I nodded. "Thanks."

He rushed from the room and returned just a few seconds later. I took the wet towel and cleaned up. It was nice of him to think of it. My ex-boyfriend, who was back-packing through Europe this year after dropping out of college—or at least that's what I thought I saw on social media—had never been that considerate. It was a small thing, but I appreciated it.

"Feeling better today?" I got out of bed, finding my pajama pants and putting them back on.

He nodded. "Yep. Particularly right now." Chance leaned over and kissed me. "You're so pretty. You know that, right?"

I'd never particularly thought of myself that way. My red hair was fine, it appealed to certain people and not others. I wasn't short or tall at five foot five inches exactly. I was rounder than was fashionable but not overweight, mostly because I jogged regularly.

I had freckles all over my body. If I disliked anything about myself it was that. Everywhere I looked, there was a spot.

"That's sweet." I patted him on the arm. "I'm sure you know what you look like."

His smile broadened. "As long as you think I'm hot, I'm good." He tugged his shirt off and walked over to his drawers. "I'm going to be out all day, picking up trash. Banyan and Maven gave up their vacation to do this with me, and I know why they're doing it. It has to be multiple members of SPiI to count toward the community service, and they don't want me overdone second semester. Between finding time for all the pledge activities we have to do and studying, I'm not at all sure how we're going to get our hours in for all of this community service if we don't use vacations. It'll be spring break, too."

I listened to what he said but all of my attention was on his back. Chance had long marks all over his back.

Thin and thick, they were raised bumps crisscrossing his skin.

"Chance, what happened?" Maybe I shouldn't have asked. Despite our physical contact, we were still in the getting to know you phase of our friendship.

His back tightened. "Usually, I remember to not let anyone see." He sighed, his shoulders slumping slightly. He turned to look at me. "I could tell you the lie I tell when I get caught. I mean, not to the guys here. My pledge class knew what happened to me, and Banyan and Maven before that because we really bonded right away. I tell people that I was in a car accident."

I nodded. The way we all had to keep our secrets was exhausting. "I can take that answer. You don't have to explain."

His gaze softened, his green eyes glistening for a second. "You wouldn't push, would you? You'd just know that I was lying to you and accept that because it would make me feel more at ease."

I touched his hand, linking our fingers together. "I'm a firm believer that we all get to keep our own secrets if we want to. Mostly, we have reasons for them."

"My father loses it a lot. My mother died when I was ten. She fell and hit her head on some ice." Chance stopping me from leaving the house this morning suddenly made a lot more sense. "I guess for years, my older brother, Jack, took the brunt of his temper. Protected me from it. I just thought Dad was a blowhard. Yelled a lot. Doesn't even drink, so that's not an excuse. Not that it would be anyway." He shook his head. "Long story short, Jack went to college when I was twelve. The next, I'd say, four years, it was my turn. After that, I was taller than he was and I grabbed that frickin whip disguised as a belt and I..." His nostrils flared.

"Let's just say it stopped. We don't see each other anymore. I don't see Jack either, which is a shame, but we both had to escape. He works for a bank in Hong Kong. I reach out sometimes. He messaged me to have a good Christmas yesterday. I'm rambling."

I squeezed his hand. "I'm so sorry."

Sometimes words were useless. There was nothing really to say that could ever make that better. Chance Montgomery. SPiI brother. Pledge Master. Future doctor. Charming smile. Flirt. He carried scars on his back that he'd never show the world. All of the girls coming in and out of his house, in and out of his life, they just wanted the external. I could see it now. Why none of them mattered.

Truth was dark. It was yucky. It was the same everywhere I went.

"I like that you know. I like I won't have to hide it."

I let him pull me in for a hug. "I'll never tell a soul, Chance."

"I know you won't. You keep your own secrets, don't you? I see them floating across your eyes when you're thinking really hard."

I had a whole bunch of them. "Do you want one of mine?"

"I..."

A knock sounded on the door. Maven called through the door, "Come on, sleepyhead. We have garbage to get out of the gardens. Sorry to wake you, Giovanna."

Chance stepped back. He walked to his closet and dressed. Jeans. A t-shirt and a sweatshirt with his SPiI letters on it. A black coat. Socks and boots. All of it was done super fast. I was impressed. I couldn't put on clothes that quickly.

He finally spoke. "Another time if you want to share, I'll

listen. It's what friends do. I'm guessing yours aren't an illustration all over your back. What will you do today?"

"The literary magazine, and I'll read. It's icy, so I guess I'm not jogging."

He pointed to the floor. "Back of the basement, behind the dance floor, there's a brown door. The gym is in there. Couple of treadmills. Bikes. Weights. Have at it. No need to worry about falling. Put on one of those pins that's on the treadmill, so if you do fall, it turns off."

I nodded. "I will. Thanks."

"See you later." He bent over to kiss me on the lips.

And just like that, he was gone. With the door open, I heard his footsteps going down the stairs; Banyan said something and then laughter; the door opening and closing. I was alone in the SPiI house.

I texted the girls. *Did everyone have a nice Christmas?*

Neither my books nor the literary entries seemed appealing. I put on my shorts, a bra, a white t-shirt, socks and sneakers before I made my way down to the basement. I stopped in my tracks. Chance had said dance floor, and he hadn't been kidding. They had a dance floor the size of a ballroom, complete with a DJ booth that was above the floor, like a box in a theater. Lights of all different colors hung from the ceiling. More rooms than I bothered to count were attached, leading who knew where. The house was huge upstairs. I should have realized the basement would be the same.

They didn't just party here... they *partied.*

I shook my head. Just when I thought I got comfortable with everything, I found myself having to readjust again. SPiI wasn't just this place where guys bonded in brotherhood and became better people than they used to be. It was where people came to party with them. There were reasons I'd designed my life to be quiet.

I was really, really bad at parties.

Well, there wasn't one at the moment. I followed Chance's instructions and found the gym. The treadmill called my name. By the time I had run three miles, I wasn't worried about the dance floor. Whatever they wanted to do was not my business. I was figuring out this friendship with the three of them, but I suspected it would have nothing to do with this.

I took the stairs two at a time and used their shower again. This time, I styled my unruly hair and tried to dress like I cared what I looked like. I wasn't always a mess. I didn't think.

The girls had answered my text, and I read their responses. Molly griped a little bit about R.J. being distracted, but otherwise, everyone was fine. Maybe she'd break up with him. I kept hoping.

It was lunchtime, and I was still not interested in what I should be doing. The main dining hall was open, so I walked over to it and bought a bunch of sandwiches. The guys needed to get hours in to make their community service happen. I'd bring them something to eat.

For a small school of two thousand people, the campus was actually quite spread out. Between the walk to the dining hall and the walk to the garden area, I added a mile to the three miles I'd traveled that day.

The gardens looked like they'd been half cleaned. Who had made such a mess of them to begin with? I could imagine the dreaded Dean Brown throwing his trash all over them just to give the guys something to do on the otherwise immaculate campus. Well, immaculate other than my burned dorm. I shuddered. I'd love to never have to get out of a building on fire again. For the rest of my life.

"Hey." Maven saw me first and waved. "Come to see us in all our glory?"

He set down the trash bag he was holding as the other two turned around. "Came to feed you."

I held up the bag I'd brought. Banyan grinned from ear-to-ear. "The woman is a goddess."

"Thank you." Maven stretched his arms over his head. "We'll take it."

"Did you walk here?" Chase pointed at me like I didn't know who the *you* referred to. "After you went to the dining hall?"

I nodded, approaching them. "Yes."

"There's ice all over the ground." A muscle ticked in his jaw. "It's dangerous, Vonni. If you fell, there might not be anyone around for hours or even days to see you needed help."

"Hey." Banyan patted his back. "She's okay. I get it. But she's okay."

Chance looked away. "Thank you for lunch. Sorry for the attitude."

That wasn't attitude. That was fear. "I stuck to the sidewalks that were salted." I lifted my left foot. "Wearing my boots. I didn't mean to frighten you. I just wanted to feed you because you guys have been feeding me."

Chance's gaze warmed. "I've clearly got an issue with this because of my mom. Thank you for lunch, Vonni."

"I know. It's okay." I handed him a wrapped sandwich.

Maven looked between us. "Glad he told you about his mom so I don't have to try to talk around why my brother here just lost his mind."

"If you want to go somewhere and there is ice on the

ground, could you call or text me? I'll come and get you, or one of these two will."

I handed Banyan and Maven their sandwiches. "Well, I could. But I don't have your cell numbers."

"That," Banyan said as he pulled out his phone, "we have to fix. Here, I'll put us all in your phone. You put yourself in mine and then share the contact with these two."

My mom liked to study moments in cultures that held significance. To do A, meant B. Like in Judaism, to have a bar mitzvah was to be considered a man. At our little college, to exchange numbers really meant we were friends. I was officially in their contact lists, and they were in mine.

"Need some help?" I pointed to the mess. "I bet after lunch, four people could clean this better than three."

I highly suspected this was so slow moving because these three SPiI brothers had never cleaned anything like this in their life. I had. For once, I could be useful to them.

SEVEN

I sat on the couch in the SPiI house next to Maven, with Banyan on my other side. Chance sat across from us, his feet up on the table. We were all pretty tired and frozen from our day outside cleaning. But the garden was beautiful now. It would bloom in the spring without any garbage to mar its beauty, assuming no one else dumped their stuff there.

"Who is keeping track of your hours?" The thought dawned on me.

Maven raised his hand. "Me. Dean Brown said he trusted me to be an upstanding human being."

Banyan laughed. "Boy did he know how to motivate you."

"I do tend to respond to people saying they trust me. I know I'm manipulated that way." He groaned. "It's like my kryptonite."

He had just made a geek reference. I grinned. "I wouldn't have pegged you as a comic book guy. Or is it just the movies?"

"You should see his room at home." Chance raised his

eyebrows. "Mister Suave here has comic books all over his room."

"A Superman reference is mild for me. If I get going, I start talking about really obscure characters only I know, and then it's all downhill from there." He nudged me. "Don't judge."

I held up my hands. "Never. Do you fudge the times at all? Like maybe you could shave ten minutes here and there."

"No." Chance shook his head. "He'd never do that. Never lies unless it's to protect someone. Never cheats. We'll do every minute and maybe ten more if he thinks there might be question about whether or not he's done it correctly."

Maven didn't argue. "Correct. They'd be the same way."

That was interesting. "What are you all going to do tonight?"

Chance smiled. "What are you going to do?"

"I'm probably going to go to a movie. That tends to be what I do. I study. I go to the movies. I read. Pretty boring." I pointed downstairs. "That's quite a dance floor you have down there."

Banyan nudged my foot. "Don't dance?"

"Not if I can help it."

Maven stood. "Looks like we're all going to the movies tonight."

"You guys don't have to. It's within walking distance and"—I made eye contact with Chance—"I'll be very careful."

Banyan put his arm around me. "Nothing for it, sweetheart. We're all going to the movies, and we're going to do this incredible thing—we're going to *drive* there because that will keep us warmer. I like my car. I only see it when I'm at school. No need for the car in the city. We're going to use mine."

"I like my car, too." Maven rolled his eyes. "And you spent most of high school in boarding school in Connecticut. You used your car there. I am the only one out of the three of us who actually spent time living in Manhattan. Having your mailing address there doesn't count. You two got to drive. I had to get my license to come to college."

Banyan shrugged. "Still driving."

They were funny. "I'm a really terrible driver. I mean really bad. I learned in Kenya, but then I didn't drive for years. I'm just horrible at it."

Chance leaned forward. "We may have to do something about that. Can't have you getting hurt."

"I almost never drive. So it's not a problem."

Maven pointed at the door. "Movies. Now. Before we all end up on this couch drinking beer, except for Giovanna with her water. And soon we'll have corrupted her into doing nothing with us except sitting on the couch on nights we don't have parties. She actually does things. Let's do them, too."

"You guys cleaned all day. It's perfectly okay to sit on the couch."

Banyan rose. "No, he's right. Let's go to the movies. When was the last time we went to the movies? Years?"

Chance shook his head. "I went last month. I took a girl out. It didn't go well. Not the movie's fault. I pissed her off when I didn't like the movie. That was some sort of personal affront."

Forty-five minutes later, I sat in the discount-for-students movie theater waiting to see the movie *French Kiss* with the three of them. For a dollar, the movie theater showed old movies once a week. I loved going, and Meg Ryan was a favorite of mine.

I wasn't sure how this was going to go over with them, but they'd bought popcorn, candy, and soda. Plus, they seemed to be laughing at the right times. At one point, Banyan leaned over to whisper in my ear. "We could be in France by tomorrow."

We'd had this back and forth already. Besides, it was amazing how much I could learn about someone in twenty-four hours. "You wouldn't leave them here to do this without you."

He squeezed my knee, and a jolt of pleasure traveled up my spine. "That's true, sweetheart. That's true. So when the community service is over in May, we could go."

"Not unless I am paying for my half." I shook my head. "Grand Canyon, remember?"

"Counting on it."

Maven threw popcorn at Banyan. "Stop. Don't talk during the movie."

So we shut up.

I'd never been to Paris. Maybe someday I would go. But it wouldn't be tomorrow. That was someone else's fairytale, not mine. I'd never wanted to be that girl swept off her feet and taken care of. I just wanted to be wanted, wherever I was. That was all I needed in life. I never wanted to be anyone's burden.

Not anymore.

I shook my head, turning my attention back to Meg. She was lost in Paris. I could think of worse places to be lost.

The sun had gone to bed by the time we came out of the movie. Maven pointed at a restaurant across the street. "I've been there. Do you like Italian, Giovanna?"

"I do, actually. As my first name might indicate, that's my mom's background. I love it."

Maven nodded, his face very serious. "Then we have to drive to Manhattan, because the Italian food here is not good Italian food."

"It's edible. It's open. The rest of the town is practically shut down until after New Year's. Let's go," Banyan answered.

Maven had been right. The food was just fine, not great, but I ate my pasta and happily listened to the three of them talk. Maven seemed to be pretty serious. He would smile and laugh, but he didn't make the jokes, which made the fact that he called me library out on the street pretty amazing. Why had he done that? Chance was charming, although every once in a while he'd get really quiet, his eyes far away. Either Maven or Banyan would bring him back to the present. Banyan made everyone laugh. He was sweet.

I fell into my usual routine, where I was comfortable: watching. If they spoke to me, I answered, but I didn't start the conversations. I actually preferred it this way. Dinner was always pressure to impress with whatever I talked about. I'd rather listen. I could learn so much more that way.

No one asked me what was wrong. No one tried to get me to talk by asking pointed questions. I hated those moments. All I had to do was enjoy.

When the check came, all three of them reached for it. I pulled out my wallet. I'd been careful with what I ordered. I had that much to spend. Maven had bought the movie for everyone, and although I'd almost objected when he did it, I'd backed off. The other two didn't seem to mind him doing it.

Banyan had the bill. "Wallet away, sweetheart."

"Banyan, you don't have to buy me dinner."

He smiled, pulling out his credit card. "You bought me lunch."

That was true. I had. I'd spent roughly the same on dinner so I put my money away. "That was a thank you."

"Are you going to fight me on the ten dollars I spent on your chicken?"

I shook my head. "Thank you for dinner, Banyan."

"You're welcome." He smiled like I'd really just given him a gift.

Chance sighed. "Thank you for dinner, Banyan."

"Aw, fuck off." Banyan threw a piece of bread at him, which made everyone laugh. "Come on. We're going home."

Home. I guessed it was for them. They'd been living in it for three years. It probably did feel like home. "Do all of the houses look like yours?"

Maven took my hand and led me toward the car. Snow fell slightly on our heads. "No. Ours is the nicest."

"Well, obviously." I laughed. "But what do the others look like?"

Chance answered. "We spend a lot of time keeping ours up. It needs paint on the outside, but we have cleaners who come after every party. It's all part of our dues. The others are varying degrees of nice and disgusting and everywhere in between. Why do you ask?"

"My roommate, Molly, is always trying to get me to go to her boyfriend's frat, DKI. I was just wondering what it looked like inside? She spends a lot of time there."

Banyan opened the door. "Who's her boyfriend?"

"His name is R.J. Winters."

Banyan groaned. "Serious douchebag."

"I hate him," Maven agreed. "Sorry. He's probably your friend right?"

"No, I hardly know him, actually." And what I did know, I didn't like. I got in the car at the same time as Chance, and Maven scooted in next to me.

Banyan got in the driver's seat and stared back at the three of us. "Are you kidding with this? One of you has to sit up front. Come on Giovanna, you're up. Sit next to me."

"You wanted to drive, man." Maven smirked. "Drive. Girl stays back here with me. She's spending the night with you. I get to sit next to her."

Chance shrugged. "She smells good. I'm not moving."

He played with the end of my hair. I watched his fingers move slightly, remembering suddenly what he'd been doing with them this morning. Heat infused my cheeks.

"Fuck." Banyan groaned. "I hate all of you."

Maven kicked the back of his seat. "You know you don't, bro. I'll get up front."

Banyan winked at me in the mirror. "Paris. Tokyo. You name it."

I winked back at him. This was just a game, and we both knew it. It didn't require a response from me. Maven got up front, and then we were off. Driving back to SPiI together like it was the most natural thing in the world for us to be doing.

"Guys, you know I'm not usually comfortable around people. I don't talk very much. I'm not sure why it's so easy with you, but I appreciate it. Feeling like this—easy, I guess —for just a short period of time is really wonderful."

Maven turned around from the front seat. "It's all because of me, library. I shouted at you on the street."

"Oh come on." Chance shifted a little until it occurred to me that I was still sitting in the middle of the backseat. That couldn't be comfortable for him. I should move across. I undid my seatbelt to move, and he grabbed my belt, rehooking it. "Don't do that. We're driving. Not safe."

"I thought you might not be comfortable having to be squished up against me. I wanted to give you more room."

He shook his head. "I don't want more room. Lean on me. Stay buckled." He put his arm around me, and I did lean on him.

I waited for a flippant remark from either Maven or Banyan, but none came. They didn't seem to react badly when Chance expressed safety concerns. Maybe they were just used to it, or maybe they understood so well what was behind it they'd never say a word. Did he tell them to be careful on the ice or was this just me?

We got back to the frat house, and they all headed up the stairs. Banyan took my hand. "You're with me tonight, unless you'd rather not be. Always up to you."

"I'm happy to come with you."

He tugged me to his side. "Great."

"I'd better get my stuff out of Chance's room." The thought dawned on me right as I said it.

Chance called over his shoulder, "I'm keeping the books."

"He's keeping your books?" Banyan shook his head. "Do you not want them anymore?"

"I read them already. We're kind of trading."

He nodded. "See you upstairs."

I grabbed my suitcase and was about to leave when Chance grabbed me by the arm, pulling me to him to kiss me lightly on the lips. "Sleep well. Banyan won't wake you up talking in his sleep."

"I didn't mind, Chance. Besides, it got me into your bed with you and then... yeah."

He ran a finger over my cheek. "Yeah." He paused like

he was going to say something else and then didn't. "See you in the morning."

I made my way up the stairs to Banyan's loft. Except it really wasn't a loft. He had the entire attic space as his bedroom. There were paintings everywhere. Half done or completed, covering the walls. His bed was against a small circular window. A second bed was in the corner of the room. It looked like he'd attempted to make both beds, but it was sort of more like the covers had been pulled up.

The bed sheets matched on both beds. They were black, like his favorite sweatshirt, which reminded me I had it. I opened my suitcase and pulled out the shirt. "Thank you for this."

He shook his head. "Keep it."

"Banyan." I walked toward him until I stood right up against him. "It's your favorite shirt. I can't keep it."

He ran a finger down my nose. "Are you going to turn down every gift I give you?"

"No." I shook my head. "But you can't give me your favorite sweatshirt. You clearly paint in it. It's all over the shirt. You might need it to make the art happen one day, and who knows if we'll know each other then."

His eyes widened. "I know we just met, but you're imagining a world where you don't know me? You fit with us. Like I know you can't live in this house with us forever, but you're just down the road. At least for the next six months. Then I'm only going back to Manhattan. That's a couple hours' drive."

"I've never really gotten to stay anywhere very long. This school is the longest I've stayed anywhere. My parents took a new job and then boom I was gone. I realize that isn't my life anymore, per se. Although I am flying out to see them this summer because they've deemed it so. I never assume I'm keeping anyone in my life."

He kissed the top of my head. "See there is this newfangled technology called phones."

I laughed, and he pulled back to grin at me. I shook my head. "It's not the same. Friendships can fade when there's no face-to-face contact. Trust me, I know."

He pointed a finger at me. "Try and get rid of me. I like you. I don't let things I like go. I'm totally selfish and spoiled." He took the sweatshirt from me. "I'll keep it because I bet it smells like you now. Roses. Is that your shampoo?"

I nodded. "It is."

I stepped away from him to look around. I loved his work when he submitted it to the literary magazine. I hadn't known I'd ever get to know him or spend the night in his bedroom for that matter. The picture he'd sent me had been a picture of a girl reading a book and the entire world exploding above her head.

The colors had blown me away. I'd hired him to do every month's edition. But his big paintings were staggeringly good. The Manhattan skyline but stained with red splotches. Why?

"I've known a lot of artists. Some like to explain their work. Some don't. Which are you?"

"Outside of my professors, no one asks me about it. The guys look. They seem to like it, but I don't have to analyze it for them. I'd love to talk about it."

I nodded. "Why the red?"

"Red's a complicated color for me. It's my favorite, if I had to pick one. It's love and blood at the same time. I was happy in New York. I knew I was a bastard. Yes, people still use that word but I didn't mind it most of the time. It wasn't until years later that I had to leave there for my so-called education that I realized what it was to be... judged. Red is love. Red is blood. Red is... power."

I loved it. "Do you show your work? You should."

"I'm going to. Well, I'm going to try to, next year. We'll see." He shrugged like it was no big deal when it clearly was.

"You're really, really talented."

He touched the back of my neck. "Thank you."

"You're welcome." Something caught my eye, and I looked over at it. He'd painted in a thin black line, it could be mistaken for black ink if I didn't see the black paint to the side of the easel. But it wasn't so much what he had used as the subject of his painting. I was pretty sure it was me.

He came up behind me putting his chin on my shoulder. "Did that all last night. Started and stopped over and over. Did your hair at first but I couldn't get the color right. I'm not all that concerned with realism, but it mattered. I just tried to capture the essence of Giovanna."

I was just me outlined in black. All of my features I looked straight ahead, my eyes down. Whatever version of me he had captured, she was pretty. "I like how you see me. It's not what I look like, but I can see how it's supposed to be, enough I recognized myself. I'm not quite so elegant." The neck alone was too graceful.

He kissed the side of my neck. "Crazy woman. It doesn't come close."

Discomfort rode me hard, and I tried not to run away. "I'm... fine to look at, I guess. I don't think about it. Without the freckles, maybe I'm cuter."

"I like the freckles. I want to count your freckles."

I shook my head. "You couldn't possibly. I think I have ten more every day."

"I'll keep a running tally."

I turned in his arms. This was probably nothing to worry about. I wasn't going to dwell on how to handle an artist making me his muse temporarily. I bet if I dug through his stuff, I'd see he painted lots of girls. I was just the one here right now.

He was gorgeous. I could probably get lost in his brown eyes if I let myself. "So they let you have the whole attic to yourself?"

"I shared a room with Maven for two years. I think he was really happy to pay to have the upstairs renovated for me from the budget for this year. From now on, it'll be the social chair's room up here."

Banyan kissed me then, so softly at first I could barely feel it. I closed my eyes and breathed him in. Goosebumps broke out all over my body. I could have him, tonight, and I didn't have to think about tomorrow. We were friends. Friends who occasionally did this.

I wrapped my arms around his neck to hold onto him, but he didn't rush. Banyan took his time, making love to my mouth. Over and over. We moved to his bed, lying down, but he still made no moves to make out more. By the time he pulled back, I was hot and needing more.

His eyes were hooded. "I want to take off your shirt and make love to those breasts."

I sat up and threw my shirt aside. I was in a pink, cotton bra. It wasn't special, but I hadn't grabbed the right things when I'd packed. I owned exactly one hot set of underwear, and I didn't have it with me.

He thumbed the top of it. "I love pink. I'm going to paint you in pink next time."

"Do you have to paint me?"

Banyan nodded. "Yes."

He unclasped my bra and bit down on my nipple. My already-on-high-alert body shuddered. I grabbed onto his back, digging my fingers into his skin. He groaned. "More like that. Please. Love it. Dig your fucking nails into me as hard as you want. I love it."

Banyan changed breasts, biting down on my other nipple. He sucked hard for a second before he raised his gaze to meet mine. "What I really want to do, sweetheart, is put my mouth on you. I want to hear you call my name over and over while my tongue brings you to orgasm. If you can be frighteningly honest, so can I."

I swallowed. "Banyan, I've never been able to get off like that. I'm just acutely aware of everything about myself during that. I'm not doing enough."

He gave me a sideways smile. "So what you're saying is you need to participate?"

"That's not exactly true. I... There's just something about that. Look, I'm screwy, and I just ruined the mood."

He shook his head. "No, this is how it gets done. I need to know what you like and you have to know that I get off on oral. If you don't, it's just because some idiot hasn't done it right on you. Allow me to make up for the previous inadequacies of your bed partners. And if you want to, then please by all means, put your mouth on my cock at the same time."

I leaned back on my elbows. "I love blow jobs."

He made a motion from his eyes toward mine. "See? I knew it. We're totally compatible in bed. Then sometimes in the not so distant future, I'm going to come deep inside of you."

I got up on my knees. "We've got to take off your pants."

"My zipper. Your teeth. I can get bossy, sweetheart, if you don't like it you're going to have to tell me."

As an answer I pulled at his jeans' button to open it before I took his zipper in my mouth. I didn't want him ordering me around on the street or if he ran into me in class but in bed? I'd take it anytime. I was hot, and wanting. He pulled at my pants, until they were off.

"Your panties match your bra."

I nodded. "Always."

I pulled his zipper with my teeth until it was down and I could take his pants off of his with a hard tug.

"This would go better if you were at that end and I'm at that other."

I smiled at him. "Not in my mouth, okay?"

"Wouldn't, sweetheart, not without permission. I'm clean but I'll prove it to you before I ask you to trust me. Next couple of days, okay? For now, I'll come on your breasts if you let me."

I would. A million times yes.

EIGHT

I loved giving blow jobs. There was so much power in that moment, to know you were solely responsible for how excited the guy got. Before I'd ever had a penis inside of me, I'd done this for months. I was good at this.

But so, it turned out, was Banyan. I wanted to give him the best head of his life but I could hardly concentrate. His tongue was doing extraordinary things. I hadn't known it could feel like this. Mostly I'd always found it uncomfortable. Not anymore.

He straddled my body, which was great because it kept my hands free to touch him everywhere I wanted to. When I couldn't get him solely down my throat, I followed with my hand. Over and over, I stroked and sucked.

Banyan moaned, the vibration moving through me and causing me to shudder. My body was alive and any hesitation I'd had about this as being uncomfortable wasn't present right now. Every cell in my body wanted this, badly.

I concentrated on what I was doing. The taste of him. Hot. Male. Wet. Salty. For the moment, all mine. I didn't have to think past now. I could just have him, I could give him pleasure and receive it in return. And oh, God, could he give it.

He didn't fumble. Banyan knew what he was doing and his tongue, so sweet when he spoke, was wicked in his ministrations. He'd bring me close and pull me back. Minute by minute, he got harder in my mouth until I could feel him throb for release.

I was close, but sometimes pleasure eluded me. Even when I craved it so much. Even when everything was right. My body fought me on what I needed. I pulled back just enough to speak to him. "I might not. Sometimes it's just me."

He moaned against me, and I shivered. "Fuck that," he managed to say. "I'm not in a hurry. I love this so much. Could do it all night, sweetheart."

The pressure was off me. I closed my eyes and just... felt. It was hard for me to get out of my own head, but I managed. My body pulsed. He didn't need me to hurry up so I didn't. And then it came, my breathing quickening. "I'm going to..."

I barely managed to get the words out.

"Yep." He jerked his hips back. "Let me out. If you are, I am."

He bit down on my clit and I exploded. Right there, in his mouth while he came on my breasts. This was hot. My body convulsed. I whispered his name in the midst of my incoherent mumblings and sighs. Colors passed in front of my closed eyelids. Banyan came on a loud shout, hard and fast. I kept my eyes closed, just concentrating on breathing. How long had we been doing that? I didn't know, didn't care.

He got off me, and I moaned, missing his warmth. I forced my lids open. Where was he going? Were we done? Was he going to want me to leave?

Banyan bent over and kissed my forehead. "Be right back. Don't move. I like you like that. Naked and relaxed. I like you every other way, too, but that's an image I'd like to repeat. Fuck, you were... yeah."

His sweet tongue was back. He tugged on his boxers and went out the door and down the stairs. As soon as he was gone, coldness invaded where the warmth had been. He'd said to stay where I was, but there was a huge difference between being naked with Banyan and naked by myself in Banyan's room. I grabbed his blanket and wrapped myself in it like a cocoon.

I was really not acting like myself lately. I was chatting up a storm to three guys I'd met on the street, and now I was indulging in all the things I missed and fantasized about with them as though it was the most natural thing in the world.

Maybe I was more myself right now than ever. Or perhaps, this time was like a step out of time. I was one of those fantasy heroines. I'd left my time and entered another dimension where I could just be. I was on vacation from all the problems that kept me from doing and saying what I wanted.

Banyan came back up the stairs and, upon seeing me, stuck his bottom lip out. "Boo. I wanted you naked and now you are covered up. Here." He held up a washcloth. "Unwrap. It's warm. I make a mess. I clean up. At least when it comes to you."

I winced. "Wasn't thinking. Made a mess of your blanket, maybe? I'll wash it with your sweatshirt as soon as I find a washer, dryer."

He shrugged, tugging at my blanket. "Hate to break it to you, but this would absolutely not be the first time I stained this thing with that particular substance. I've had this blanket since I was thirteen. So, yeah. I'll wash it. Not washing the sweatshirt. It smells like you. Oh, come to think of it so will this. Hmm."

I let him unwrap me and gently clean me off. Embarrassment had me moving toward my suitcase for clothes. My inhibitions hadn't gotten the message that they had to stay away until January 7th.

"Change your mind." He walked over to grab another cover out of his closet before he lay down on the bed. "Let's sleep naked, skin-to-skin. Honestly, it'll be a first for me. I kick girls out most of the time. I'm an asshole. But, I want to with you tonight. If you do. Or get dressed. Whatever you want."

He'd known exactly what I was going to do. Then again, I'd hardly been subtle making a beeline for my bag. I twisted up my face. "I'd love to keep looking at you naked, but I'm feeling exposed."

There was the honesty again. I had to keep it up. Retreating into my sures and fines didn't work this week. Not on my vacation from my life.

Banyan patted the bed. "Come here."

He lifted the cover, this one a plaid brown and blue quilt, and I got under it with him. "This is new. It's fun. It's crazy this is happening so easily. You're maybe the coolest girl I've ever met. Even the ones who come here and are okay with being passed around are ultimately hoping one of us will fall for them and date them. There's the whole lettering ceremony, where they get the shirt. A pinning if they're practically engaged. I'm going on and on here. The point is that you will eventually not worry about being naked. You'll know I'm so hot for you that I frickin' love it. That's all."

I leaned up on my elbow. These girls wanted to be pinned and lettered by the fraternity. To be recognized by the entire brotherhood as belonging to their boyfriend. "Do the sororities do anything similar? And your boxers are still on while I have to be naked?"

He gave me a sheepish smile. "Whoops." Banyan threw his boxers across the room. "There, now we're equal. As for your other question," He shook his head. "No, they don't. There's a lot of cache to getting lettered in the sororities, or so I'm told. Those ladies earn their letters too, but they'll stop wearing their own to wear ours. Whatever. We're supposed to vote on whether or not we want to let a brother give over his letters. I never say no. I mean, what the fuck; his girl, his life. She has to give them back if they break up. Did you ever think about rushing?"

I shook my head. "I remember when Miranda did. She was my freshman year roommate. She hated me. It was a lot of fuss. She was coming in and out in the middle of the night. I had a freshman year seminar I had to get through. Even if I could have tolerated the idea of giving so much time away from my studies—and I have to be hyper-vigilant or I don't pass—I don't have the money."

He took my hand in his. "Really glad you didn't, actually. We'd have a very different relationship right now. There would be things you would think you would know about me, and things I would think I knew about you. Only about fifty percent of the time is any of that accurate."

I sighed. "That app."

His eyebrows shot up. "You know about that app? Did you look at it?"

"No, my roommate's boyfriend, R.J., suggested I look at it when he heard I was staying here."

Banyan rolled over onto his stomach, tugging me until I lay by his side. "He would say that. Considering DKI spends half their time writing bullshit about all of the other frats in that fucking thing. They post all the time, flood all other postings out of view. They all look like saints, and we're all drunken lunatics. Not just SPiI, but every other house on campus. They rate the sorority girls, too. Call them fat. Ugly. Sluts. It's not cool."

No, it really was not. "I hate those words. I hate anything that labels us as other and therefore bad. Or less than." Stupid was my least favorite ever. I'd almost rather be called anything else.

"You wore me out. That hot mouth of yours. Damn, sweetheart, I don't remember the last time I came that hard."

I smiled at him. "Thanks. You were pretty hot there yourself."

"My head is drifting. I'm going to pass out. Most nights I have nightmares. You saw me after one. But I won't wake you. I'm quiet about it."

I almost asked him if he wanted to talk about it, but he'd just told me he wanted to sleep. "Do you sleep with the light on?"

He shook his head and clapped his hands. The lights went out. "I'm lazy."

I laughed. Banyan was fun and sweet. There were much worse ways to spend the night.

I closed my eyes.

It felt like I'd only been asleep a few minutes when I heard the sirens. Fire trucks. I gasped. We had to get out. If there was a fire, then we had to get out. I had to run. Grab my shoes. Get out of the dorm. Wait. Where was I? Where was the fire?

"Sshh." Banyan tugged me closer. "I hear them. It's not here. Close, but not here. I've got you." He kissed my cheek. "You're safe, sweetheart, you'll always be safe with me. I promise. No fire."

I nodded. Yes, now that my head was clearing from sleep, I could tell he was right. The alarms weren't here. Banyan scooted out of the bed, pulling a new pair of boxers out of his dresser and sticking them on. He followed with a t-shirt. Then his pants and a sweater. We should get dressed. I swung my legs over the bed.

"Stay here, okay? I'm going to go find out what's happening, but you should stay here. It's snowing out there. Stay warm."

He grabbed his coat and bent over to kiss my cheek. "Go back to sleep. You're safe. I'll be right back."

Banyan left the room before I could truly make my mind turn on. There was another fire? Maven had said someone lit the laundry room of my dorm on fire but I'd thought it was some drunk asshole being stupid. Another fire? Was someone doing this on purpose?

I got out of bed and dressed myself in my pajamas. Flannel pants and a white t-shirt weren't sexy, but they were warm. I didn't want to be naked if this place went up next. I threw on my sneakers and walked to the window. The fraternity house closest to Brentwood Avenue was ablaze. I gasped. We'd been lucky in our dorm. Was anyone there in that house? I pressed my fingers to the window just as my phone beeped across the room.

I ran over. Maven had texted me. *It's the Alpha house.*

No one there over the holiday. Stay inside. It's a mess out here.

Tears flooded my eyes. Whatever was happening, it needed to stop. Someone was going to get hurt. I'd never given fire the slightest thought. I'd seen flood, famine. I'd witnessed suffering all over the planet. I somehow had been spared fire, and now it was burning up my wealthy college campus.

I texted Maven. *I could come help you do whatever you're doing.*

He responded right away. *Not doing anything. Coming right back. No one to help. Firemen are doing their jobs.*

Well, there went that idea. I clapped my hands to turn on the lights, and then grabbed one of my books and sat down on Banyan's bed. I'd taken this story from Chance, and it seemed like a good premise. I couldn't get into it since it was hard to tell if the narration was horrible or the world was burning down and so I couldn't concentrate.

It didn't matter. Banyan appeared a few seconds later, throwing off his shoes and his coat before plopping down on the bed. He clapped his hands, and the lights went off.

We hadn't spoken a word, and yet he curled up against me on the bed. I dropped my book onto the floor and rolled toward him.

"That house is gone. And one of the firemen said it was an incredibly fast blaze." His voice was low. Through his curtains, I could see flashing lights on the streets. The lights of the crews trying to save what they could. Heroes. They ran in where people ran out.

"Banyan, this is the strangest winter vacation of my life."

He nodded. "Me, too. But not all in a bad way. I mean... a lot of it has been fantastic."

We fell asleep just like that, both of us fully dressed with the lights outside his window flashing and blinking.

The bed dipped and woke me. Banyan groaned, and I forced my eyes open. Light streamed into the room, bright— not like the early morning but like the afternoon. How long had we been asleep?

We hadn't moved. We were still both above the covers. What was happening?

Maven sat on the end of the bed, leaning on the wall. "Afternoon sleepyheads. Sorry to wake you."

Banyan rubbed his face. "What in the ever loving fuck, man? I let you sleep. We don't have to rush over to sort the Dean's papers today. Give me a break. And she was terrified last night. You had to wake her?"

Maven patted my leg, his hand staying on it after the third pat. "I'm sorry. I was sleeping, too. But we got a text from Dean Brown. He's emptying the campus while they figure out what's going on. We have to leave. No students on campus by 3 p.m. It's one. We have to go."

A cold emptiness filled my gut. Well, so much for my vacation from myself. I was going to have to figure out what to do.

Banyan sat up slowly. "Do you need any help getting the house secured?"

"Nope. I got it. Chance just got up and made coffee. See you guys downstairs. We aren't getting any more community service hours done this week. Guess it's Manhattan for New Year's."

The artist in the room groaned. "I have a plane at my disposal. We can be more creative than home."

I rose. This was a discussion for them to have amongst themselves. I had to shower and get packed. Hopefully the hotel had rooms, or else I was getting in a taxi and going a little bit further than I wanted. How could the dean just kick us off campus? When I'd taken the college tour, my father had specifically asked if students could remain in the dorms over holidays. Internally, I groaned at the memory. I'd been so embarrassed. He'd actually said that we needed a place because I was going to be expected to manage on my own a lot.

That had been news for me.

I turned to Maven. "Do I have time to shower?"

He nodded, his gaze caressing my body. "Sure. Cute pajama pants. I like how you're always in flannel."

I shrugged. "I don't own any lingerie."

"That so?" He got to his feet. "See you in a bit. Banyan, don't fall back asleep."

"I'm up."

I grabbed my stuff. It made the most sense to bring the entire suitcase down to the bathroom with me rather than traipsing around at this point. Banyan hummed to himself—grabbing things, packing up his art supplies—when I left the room. I kept the shower brief. It was better not to wash my hair every day, so I focused on cleaning the rest of me. I dried myself quickly and got dressed in a pair of jeans that I paired with a red sweater that was slightly too big on me. I didn't love my clothes clinging to my curves.

I threw on my black boots, and I was ready to go. I just needed to say goodbye to the three guys who had been so nice to me when I'd been desperate. It wasn't the middle of the night, I had my stuff, and I was going to be fine after I figured out if the hotel had space for me.

"Hey guys," I called out as I made my way down the stairs. "Thank you so much for everything."

Chance leaned against a wall, drinking his coffee. Banyan sat on the couch, his elbows on his knees, and

Maven sat on the table in the living room rather than the chair. They all stared at me.

Chance answered. "Why do you sound like you're saying goodbye?"

"Because I'm saying goodbye." Wasn't that clear? "We have to leave. I'm going to call the hotel and see if they have a room. If not, I'll call all the places nearby until I find one. I'll take a taxi. I won't walk."

I would miss Chance's concern for my well-being on the ice. I came across as pretty self-sufficient and most people accepted that I was. Only, it could be lonely always taking care of just myself and having no one checking after me.

"And..." I smiled. "I will say hello if I see you guys. I promise not to do the not seeing people thing when it comes to the three of you."

Maven jumped off the table. "You're not going to that hotel. You're coming with us."

Banyan spoke right after him. "Unless we've pissed you off or you'd prefer your own company. We want you to come with us."

They did. I opened and closed my mouth. It was one thing to have this vacation from myself here in the SPiI house on campus, another for them to bring me home.

"Look, you guys just met me. You don't have to be responsible for me. I can manage."

Chance looked at Maven. "She feels like she's intruding."

"Got that." Maven nodded. "Giovanna, please come to New York with us until January 7th? If you hate it or whatever, I will put you in a town car and you can come to the shitty hotel then."

I took a steadying breath. Just when I thought I understood things, I didn't. I had to say something. "Are we going to go see the ball drop on New Year's in Time Square?"

"No," all three of them answered at once.

Chance walked over and took my hand. "That's a holy shit on toast hell of a mess. We'll do something fun. It won't be that. We're going to stay at my house."

"You're sure your father won't mind?" And I wasn't exactly sure we should go to his house considering his father's violent history.

Banyan laughed. "His father isn't going to know a damned thing about it."

Chance ran his thumb slowly down the side of my face. "When my grandmother died, she left her Upper Eastside townhouse to me, and most of her personal money to go with it. Some was allotted to the care of the cats she loved. It's a long story. Anyway, I don't ever have to sell it. I want to fix it up. It's huge and old and... it needs some work, but it's beautiful. When I get done with school and I'm established in a medical practice, I'm going to fix it up. Well, hire someone to fix it."

"I..." That was entirely different. "If you don't think it'll be too much trouble, then I'd love to go."

He grinned and stepped back. "Then it's settled. She's coming."

Maven clapped his hands together. "She's driving with me."

Chance nodded. "I'm going to get on the phone in the car with the pledge president and get him going with starting to fundraise to replace what the Alpha guys lost in the fire."

Banyan patted Chance on the back. "Good call. And I'm thinking a two dollar cover to come in the house on the 7th for the back to school party. All proceeds go to Alpha."

"Get to it, guys." Maven took my arm. "See you in Manhattan in a couple of hours."

He ushered me to his car, and I got in. I really knew little about cars, but this one looked expensive and it smelled new. My mind wandered away from the real. In this book, I was the heroine with some extraordinary talent being brought to New York City to perform, but I'd really just miss my small town routes. The only problem with my leaving was that I'd gone and fallen in love with...

No, I had to stop the daydream. I didn't do romance daydreams. They were too problematic, and my heart sometimes couldn't separate the fantasy I had with real life. I'd suddenly be crushing on someone who didn't know I was alive.

What was happening here was exciting enough. "I feel a little bit like I've just gone down a rabbit hole."

"Why, sometimes I've believed as many as six impossible things before breakfast," Maven quoted from the book I'd been referencing. He pulled away from the house, driving slowly over the street. "The car is four wheel drive and the roads are salted, but I'm going to take it easy until we get on the highway."

I needed to come up with something to say. It was easier with Maven, Banyan, and Chance than it had been with others, but sometimes I couldn't seem to function like others did. "I'm a terrible driver. I wouldn't worry about me judging you. We'd be in a ditch if it were me. Um, I never asked you your major. You're pre-law, obviously."

"Pre-law is a certificate. Finance major." He smiled at me. "Breathe, Giovanna. Hard to talk all the time. I'll make conversation, and then you can tell me to stop if you get enough. Been to New York City before?"

I nodded. "Sure. Three times. But very quick in and

out. We caught *Annie* on Broadway, and I took the Staten Island Ferry to see a view of the whole city."

Maven raised his eyebrows. "You like Broadway?"

"I liked Annie." I didn't have a huge amount of experience with other shows.

He grinned. "Broadway we can do."

NINE

I must have dozed off in the car because I woke up when we were crossing the George Washington Bridge. Maven had sports radio playing low. They were talking about two players who were out because they were injured. I rubbed my eyes.

"Sorry, I haven't been good company in the car."

"You don't have to apologize for sleeping. In fact, unless you do something really horrific, you don't have to apologize to me ever." He took my hand. "We are going to get some good Italian food in twenty-minutes. Just you and me. Okay?"

I adjusted the blow of the air in the car so that it hit me just a little less. "The other two won't mind?"

"Banyan stops for chili at a New Jersey diner anytime he makes the trip. Chance won't mind. He's got some stuff to handle."

"I'd love dinner." I was starving, having eaten nothing since I got up. "I think that sounds like fun."

"I think so, too." He smirked. "And I don't usually find most things fun. Not really. I can be amused for periods of time. Sometimes things are funny. But the majority of my time, I am sort of bored." He winced. "I can't believe I told you that."

I raised my eyebrows. "I'm... I'm not a very exciting person."

"You're honest. You're funny. You're kind. Those are not qualities I run into a lot. I'm glad we can be friends."

I felt the same way. But would we reach a point where I was as dull to Maven as everything else? "Clearly, you don't get bored with Chance and Banyan."

"They're my brothers." He drummed on the steering wheel. "And not just because we wear the same three letters on our chest."

WE'D LEFT the car in a parking lot near Chance's home and taken a taxi over to eat. Apparently, Maven's favorite place to eat Italian was on the other side of town. The restaurant Maven chose wasn't fancy. It was small inside, felt more like a European bistro. Waiters wore dark suits and spoke in what sounded like real Italian accents. I'd been through Italy once, but we'd been in a hurry. Dad spoke at a conference there, and then we'd rushed back to Greece where Mom was guest lecturing for a series of presentations.

I scanned the menu, the letters jumping around a little bit. I bit my bottom lip, a habit from childhood I'd tried to stop but sometimes still did when I was nervous. I'd compensated for my dyslexia very early and managed to learn to read when I was six. I think I did it out of sheer terror that my parents would use the word stupid again. The first time they'd done it had been when I was four. *I don't think she's stupid, Jo. I think she's just... slower.*

My brain needed to get with the program and pick something to eat. It could have been the prices that threw me off but I couldn't make a choice. How much was pasta? This was going to be a salad night. I'd been a child when I came here last; I hadn't thought about cost. New York City had a reputation for being super expensive.

I was going to have to be careful. The part time job idea was certainly going to have to become a reality. I didn't mind. I knew how to work hard. I'd just stay up later, studying. Bright side was that meant more coffee.

I'd be one of those heroines from an old television movie that I watched late at night. Really pushing through. I'd had a pretty cushy life, when it came down to it. Maybe my parents weren't everything I wished they could be, but I wanted for nothing. I didn't get to live like my three new friends, but that was okay. I was sure that came with its own set of problems.

The waiter came by, and I glanced up. Was that fast, or had I been staring at the menu without speaking for a long time? Heat traveled up the back of my neck. Maven watched me, his head slightly tilted before he looked at the server.

"I'm going to have a glass of the 2014 Honig, and she's going to have..." His voice trailed off.

"Just water." I smiled at the waiter. "Thanks."

He left to go get our drinks, and Maven closed his menu. "I'm going to assume you don't want to drink unless you tell me otherwise."

I couldn't imagine wanting one. "Thanks."

The small smile Maven sometimes gave me crossed his face. "What are you going to eat?"

"I think a salad is good tonight."

He leaned forward. "Salad is so not what you should order here."

There was something about Maven that made me always want to do what he said. Maybe it was the way that he looked at me, the intensity of his eye contact, or the fact that, so far, he'd not told anyone to do anything that wasn't really in their best interest. "You use your power for good."

He shook his head. "I'm not following."

"That power you have to get people to do what you want, you use it for good."

His smile was huge. "Aha, I have a superpower. Cool, I'll take it."

"Salad is what I can afford here if I'm going to make it to the 7th."

His grin fell. "Giovanna." He always made my name sound musical. "I'm paying. We'll all be paying from now until we leave. Don't make the same argument you keep making with Banyan. It's done."

It would have been easy to just give in. I hadn't been kidding when I called it a superpower. "I appreciate that, but friends don't pay for friends."

"They do when they bring them here. This puts you under no obligation for anything. I just want to eat here with you. That's all. End of story."

I sat back in my chair. "I wasn't worrying about owing you. Just not wanting you to feel like you had to. I think I'm going to get a part time job when I get back to school." I looked at my menu. "I'd like the ravioli."

"In the vodka sauce it's like heaven in your mouth." He took a sip of his water. "I don't have to do anything. That's the truth of my life. I'm a rich college student with a father serving time. I'm pretty much given a wide berth to make personal decisions that people don't push on too much."

I didn't know if this was something I should comment on or not. Still, he'd said it. I couldn't just ignore it. "That's not how I see you. I mean, granted we don't know each other that well."

The drinks arrived, and we ordered our food. Maven took a sip of his wine. "How do you see me?"

"Smart. Strong. Kind. A natural leader. Considerate. Generous. Funny. Outgoing. Insightful. Empathetic. You're always watching everything around you. You're good at reading people. You don't wait to see what's going to happen, you jump into action."

He held up his hand to stop me. "I'm pretty much how I described myself to you."

I took a long drink of my water. Who was I to tell Maven who he was? No one really knew me, not even myself, particularly.

He set down his drink. "Fuck."

I winced. "I've ruined dinner. I'm..." I wasn't supposed to apologize to him, so I quit halfway through that statement.

"No." He reached across the small table to touch my chin. "I want to be all those things. I want to not go to jail. I want to not fuck up the lives of everyone I encounter."

My heart beat really fast. Maven's eyes were big. I'd really struck a nerve. "I can't see you doing any of those things. That's not your story. That's not how it plays out."

"I really want to kiss you right now."

I leaned forward and moved his wine out of the way, and he took that as the consent it was. He kissed me, gently and then firmer. I closed my eyes. It wasn't a long caress, but it lit my blood on fire. He pulled back, his voice low. "I'm so happy you walked by on the street."

I was too.

We separated, and the food came soon after. It was early and they must have wanted us out to seat the next crew that would come after us. I took a bite of my ravioli. Maven had been right; it was heaven in my mouth. But all I could think about was that kiss and what would happen next.

We were quiet while we ate. I brought my gaze over to the other patrons in the restaurant. I had a hard time keeping my mind where it belonged, and other people's stories were one of my favorite distractions.

Maven followed my gaze. "Is he doing something interesting?"

Heat traveled up my neck. "Not really. I have... a problematic mind. I think something went wrong when I was being formed. Um, I can't help it, really, but I silently make up stories for people around me. Sometimes I even do that when I'm concentrating on something else. Like I can actually have more than one thing happening in my mind."

There, now he could understand exactly what being friends with me entailed.

Maven sipped his wine. He'd been slow drinking it. When he stopped, he licked his lips, and it was everything I could do to not pull him to me for another kiss. The only problem was we had dishes on the table now.

"So what's he doing? The man there, in this story you've invented for him?"

I couldn't speak for a second. "You want me to tell you what story I made up?"

"Yes. Completely. In your not screwed up brain." He nodded toward the man. "Tell me."

"See how he hasn't taken off his coat? Immediately, I think that he's on the run." As soon as I said it I wished I hadn't. Maven was going to think this was dumb. He was probably expecting insightful remarks, and I was giving him fiction.

He nodded, furrowing his brow. "Because it really is not cold in here considering it's December. It's a little hot, actually."

"Right. So he might have to run. I mean, in real life that's a job issue or a family concern. Or he has to get to the airport. In my mind, it's something different."

Maven steepled his hands. "Like what?"

"Spy novel. He's really here listening in on the couple over there who work for the Russians. He'll have to dash when they do, so he has to be ready. He plays with his food, pays early." I shrugged.

"Giovanna, I love how your mind works."

That was sweet but ridiculous. "Don't be too impressed. I think about this stuff all the time. I..." Was I going to tell him how bad it really was? I wanted to. It would be nice to say it aloud once, and this was a vacation from reality. I was in New York City with the president of SPiI. If I had my way, I was going to have sex with him that evening. Why not just be truthful for once in my damned life? "I make myself the heroine in stories. I get in a car, it's a story. I go for a jog, it's a story. I do laundry. Story. I'm dyslexic and everything is hard in school, so why not go ahead and make it harder by living this strange internal fantasy life?"

He was silent. There, I had done it now. Total turn off. I'd never be having sex tonight, and I'd be lucky if Maven didn't put me in the Town Car and send me home now. I couldn't meet his gaze. It would be too penetrating.

"Have you considered that you might be a writer?"

I stopped. "What?" I raised my eyes.

"Have you considered that the reason your brain is so anxious to make up stories when you might be better served doing other things is that you really are supposed to be telling stories? Like typing them out and maybe publishing them? You're bored because you're not doing what you were designed to do."

No, I had really not considered that, ever. "Write fiction?"

"Sure. Why not? People love fiction. If your stories are good, I bet someone would read them. I don't know about making a living. Truth is, I don't know what kind of money authors make. But you could do it part time, right? Teach writing. Some kind of sales job. I'm just throwing stuff out, but I don't think it's screwed up, Giovanna. I think it's talent."

Talent? "I never considered it. My parents are academics, and... I always just thought what they did, which is that I'm made wrong. In all kinds of ways."

His gaze flared for a second, his blue eyes flaring. "Your parents told you that you were made wrong? Those words?"

"They told it to each other when they thought I couldn't hear. But they also showed it to me just about every way possible. They're super smart. Unbelievably so. I think they thought that together they would make Einstein. But they just made me."

He drummed his hands on the table. "Well, then they made better than they deserved." He shook his head. "Our families can really fuck us up. They don't even mean to. They're all just screwed up people themselves. Terribly flawed, battling their own shit all the time. At the end of the day we are, to an extent, what they made us to be. As they were."

The bill came, and he quickly handed his credit card to the server. "I'm pretty pissed right now at your parents. I realize I've never met them, but fuck them. Seriously."

I had never, not in my entire life, had anyone take my side in a story against my parents. All I ever heard was that they were wonderful people, so incredible for society, the benefits their understanding of how societies evolved would help the world. My father was funny, with a mind that didn't stop. My mother was beautiful, focused, and brilliant.

And no one had ever said they weren't good parents. Not ever. When it came down to it, there was no one to notice, none who would care. We had no family. They'd both been only children with parents who were deceased before I was born. Who cared how they raised me? I was homeschooled until high school, and then I was just... off.

The newness of Maven's defense of me, of his immediately dislike of them rode me all the way to the street. He was about to hail us a cab when I threw my arms around him. He was warm against the night air, but even more than that, Maven was real. He rolled around in problems and didn't seem bothered or freaked out that I had some of my own.

"Thank you."

He pressed his cheek against the top of my head. "You're welcome. Fuck them."

Someone else might have thought I was hugging him as appreciation for dinner, but not Maven. I had a feeling he misunderstood very little in life.

We didn't speak in the taxi. I looked out the window as New York City passed by my eyes, not really seeing it. I was too aware of the man next to me. His hand was around my shoulders, and he rubbed exposed skin between my shoulder and my neck. Electricity shot up my spine, and I trembled. He bent over to whisper in my ear. "I'm so fucking hard right now from wanting you. You've hardly touched me, and I'm ready to beg for you."

I turned slightly until we were close enough to kiss, but I didn't make the move. "The anticipation is excruciating, right?"

"Hmm." He didn't answer with a word, more a sound from his throat. "You know it's your choice right? You can say no. I'm not..."

I kissed his lips as gently as I could. "I think it was me who introduced the idea of this to begin with. I want it. But thank you for making sure."

We got to what must have been the address. After paying the guy, Maven practically flew out of the taxi, tugging me with him. I looked up. Chance's grandmother's home was surprising. This was New York City. I thought of tall buildings. This looked more like a home. The whole block was one brownstone townhouse lined up against another. I gave a cursory glance around. That must be the style in this area.

Maven let us in, flipping on the lights as he did. "Banyan and I have the keys. If we need to get away from our mothers, we come here, whether Chance is here or not. So much so that we each officially have a room."

I stopped where I stood and looked around. There were energies to places, and this one felt like it welcomed me in. Everything was fancy and old. Chance must not have redecorated at all. This was his grandmother's stuff.

Maven kissed my cheek. "Look around. I can see I've lost your attention for a minute. Give it back to me soon. I'll be up at the top of the second staircase. The room has green and gold wallpaper."

"I don't want to just poke around. That's not polite."

He shrugged, taking the steps two at a time. "We don't care all that much about polite. Be nosy. Chance would tell you the same."

I took a second. Okay, so Maven had gone up, and he wanted me to explore? I walked quietly, like I might get in trouble for being places I hadn't officially been shown. Next to the main entrance way was a formal dining room. White chairs with green linings surrounded a white table. In the corner of the room, a spiral staircase led upward. How many staircases did this place have? I kept looking. Room after room stuffed with beautiful, antique furniture caused me to pause and inhale.

Chance wanted to update this place, and I was sure there were a ton of reasons to do so, but this was gorgeous. Hopefully, some of the stuff would stay. I lost track of bedrooms. Didn't most homes in New York City have very few?

The door to Maven's green and gold room was open. I walked in slowly. He sat on the bed, his feet crossed one over the other. His shirt sleeves were rolled up over his elbows, and two of the buttons on his shirt were undone. He looked comfortable, sexy, and just a little intimidating. He fit in this house. So would Chance and Banyan.

I didn't. But that was okay. It didn't matter tonight.

He raised his eyebrows. "You came through with confidence, and then you lost it. Green and gold wallpaper throw you off?"

I smiled at him. "It's totally the green and gold wallpaper. Nothing to do with how sexy you are on that bed. You look like... you belong here. Like you could live in this world."

He got up on his knees and extended his hand to me.

"Who gives a shit about any of it? Close the door and come here."

I did as he said, grabbing his hand when I was close enough to do so. Maven's hands were smooth, his thumb running over the top of mine where they clasped. He drew me to him.

"You could fit anywhere you wanted to. You have skin like porcelain. Big, expressive brown eyes. Your hair is like the sun setting in the Caribbean. You keep your head down, so you don't notice that others see you. All the time. I watched it over and over when you came out of the library at the same time I left my meetings. Well, I noticed you, too. I was part of the crowd. I want you. So badly. You seem to want the same. So don't get shy on me now, gorgeous."

That was a lot for Maven to say. I smiled at him before I pushed him back in the position he'd been in when I came in the room. "This is crazy you know. This friendship we have that leads to this. And we're both fine with it. Where's the drama? Where's the fuss?"

He smirked. "We'll keep that for between the sheets."

"Good answer."

I straddled him, and he sucked in his breath. We were still clothed, but I could feel his hardness pressing against me. His gaze changed, his eyes hooding slightly. I ground against him before I lifted myself off.

He widened his eyes as his hands came onto my arms, rubbing his fingers over my shirt. I did the movement again, and he made the slightest moan in the back of his throat. Yes, it felt good to me too, but seeing what I did to him was the hottest part. Over and over, I pressed against him and then pulled away.

His moans got louder, and soon he pulled my head to his, embracing me with his lips. His hands were in my hair.

I didn't stop moving. This was fun and unexpected. I hadn't anticipated that I'd want to start like this.

He pulled back. "Clothes off. Now."

I gave him my best naughty smile. Of course I was going to do what he wanted. It was hard to deny Maven anything when I wasn't caught in the throes of his heat. But I was going to play with him first. Did anyone tease Maven? "Oh really? You want me naked? You're sure."

He practically growled before he flipped me over, his body held off of mine just a little bit. He turned his head to the side, kissing my chin, my nose. "I want you naked."

"Then I guess you should get me naked."

He tugged at my top, pulling it over my head. I'd put on a nude bra and panties that matched it, but he hadn't seen those yet. It was a front clasp, and he undid it fast, throwing it aside. I grabbed at his shirt. "Take it off."

Maven winked at me. "You want it off. Take it off me."

I undid the rest of his buttons, glad my hands were steady since I didn't feel that way at all. I had to unroll his sleeves to really pull the shirt off, but soon we were skin to skin. I ran my hand over his defined abs, feeling his muscles jump under my fingers when I touched him.

He sucked in a breath, his nostrils flaring, before he took my breast in his mouth. After a second, he sucked on my nipple to the point of pain. I cried out. The bite of it, the sense that it could hurt more but didn't because it was so damned hot made my hips buck against him.

Maven kissed me, hard. Once. Then twice. I melted against him, and he sucked on my other breast. I could hardly breathe for wanting him. I dug my fingers in his back so hard it was going to leave a mark.

We pulled at each other's pants until we were both naked. His cock was hard, erect, and huge. I reached out to stroke him, a long tug from his balls all the way to the tip. He closed his eyes. "Careful. I'm so hot for you I can't see straight. I'm not coming in your hand tonight but inside your pussy."

I wanted that, too. "Do you have a condom?"

That was a question I should have asked earlier. He groaned his yes before he reached for a drawer next to the bed and pulled out a condom. His hands trembled, and he shook his head. "Damn, I'm really... on right now. I..."

I took the package from him. He didn't need to explain. I tore it open and handed it back to him. He'd have to get it on. I'd never done that, and I didn't want to screw it up. He managed quickly, and I watched, transfixed. Maven was a beautiful man.

Then he was on top of me again, this time his forehead pressed to mine. I closed my eyes. This was the part that was always the problem for me. I had to relax or it was going to be a strain getting him inside. He was a big man.

"Hey, look at me." His voice was low in my ear. "Keep your eyes on mine, okay?"

I nodded, opening my lids. "Just trying to make sure I'm completely relaxed so this doesn't go badly."

"Not possible any of this is going to go that way, gorgeous. I'm going to take such good care of you." He reached between us, finding my clit and stroking it. I cried out from the unexpected touch. "Yes, you like that. I do, too. You are going to be hot and ready for me. I promise you."

His words were a salve to whatever anxiety I had left. I was ready for him, and he knew it. Maven pressed inside of me gently. My body didn't need him to wait. I was ready. He'd no sooner pushed in than he pulled out. We cried out together. He did it again, our moans once again in sync. In and out, his body took mine again and again. I kissed him, hard, biting down on his lower lip. Maven grinned at me, his jerks getting stronger. I wanted every piece of him. I craved the end of this, but I couldn't let it be over too fast.

Not when it was so fucking perfect.

I wrapped my legs around him tighter, drawing him deeper. He grabbed onto my thigh, pushing it as far as it could go until my leg was practically on his shoulder. "Yes," I told him. This was the penetration I needed from him. He could take me as deep was he wanted. There was no such thing as too much.

Over and over, we joined and separated until I panted for him. I would have begged for release, but it didn't take that long. He hit all the right spots, seemed to know my body like we had done this many times before.

"Maven," I didn't even know what I asked for but I needed it. "Please. Please. Please."

I came hard and seconds later he did, too, my name a sigh on his lips.

I closed my eyes. Life really didn't get much better than this.

TEN

Maven liked to cuddle. Under the blankets, he touched me everywhere he could reach until he seemed to get me into a position he liked. I was like putty in his hands. I'd do whatever he liked right then. Once he had me settled, he let out a long sigh.

"I want to just pass out right here, but any second now, Banyan is going to come through the door downstairs, followed a few minutes later by Chance, and my nap would be short lived. That will make me all grumpy. I feel too good to be grumpy."

I guessed that meant I wasn't getting a nap either. "How do you know?"

"All these years together, and actually sharing a room with Banyan for three of them, means I can predict him pretty well. I just know Chance's schedule."

His phone beeped, and he rolled over, groaning. "Yep. Banyan's here. He wants us downstairs. Says he got something. Fuck. That could be anything from a new jacket to a puppy. If it's a puppy, you can't let us keep it. We'll all want to keep it, and that'll be bad because we don't have room in our life right now for a puppy."

I touched his shoulder. "I won't let you keep the puppy."

He turned around to kiss my lips. "Am I rambling?"

"You're adorable. Little stream of consciousness. It's cute."

Maven groaned. "I've got to cut it out before I go back down there." He held me for just a second. "Are we good?"

I didn't understand. "In what sense?"

He smiled at me, a big toothy grin. "Giovanna." He smoothed my hair off my forehead. "We just had sex. And I know we made this arrangement and said we were all good with it and we would be friends. I want to make sure you're still okay?"

This time, it was my turn to smile. "Because we had sex? Oh, I know this novel. This is where I get all goopy, and I'm not really okay with the arrangement I made myself because I've tied sex with emotion, and because we had sex I have to be... overwhelmed?"

Maven nodded. "I'm thinking you're fine."

"I'm really glad that we're becoming good friends. And that was amazing. My body is buzzing from it. But I'm okay Maven. I like you. I think you like me, too. Otherwise..."

He kissed my cheek. "Yes. I like you. Buddy. Pal." He laughed as he let me go. "Just when I think I've got a grasp on who you are, I don't."

A pounding on the door had me grabbing for the covers. Banyan's voice came through. "Hurry up. I've got something."

Maven smiled at me. "You know we could be naked. Like right in the middle of something."

"If Giovanna is naked, I might just forget about what I have downstairs and come in to play."

Maven threw his pillow at the closed door. "You weren't invited. We'll be right there."

I grabbed my clothes, and Maven turned to me once more. "No puppies. No cats. No birds or fish. Nothing I have to feed. I'll change my mind when I see it. Don't let me."

I shook my head. "Maven, I don't know that I can stop you from doing anything at all. If you want the animal, I'm pretty sure you'll get to keep it."

"Don't be silly, Giovanna. I think you'd be the only person in the world who could."

What did he mean by that? I never got to ask him. Banyan pounded again. What in the world did he have downstairs?

CHANCE CAME through the door just as Maven's mouth fell open. The owner of this house set down a couple of brown bags by the door and stared at what Banyan had brought into his place. "A margarita machine?"

Banyan beamed. "Yep. Awesome right? I thought we'd try it here and then bring it back to SPiI with us."

"A margarita machine? Where did you even get one?" Chance walked over to me and tugged me against his side. "Did they show you around, Vonni?"

"I showed myself around. Hope that was okay. Maven thought you'd be okay with it."

Chance squeezed my shoulder. "Maven was right. All right, we have a margarita machine. Do we have anything to make margaritas with?"

Banyan pointed to a large black duffel on the floor. "We do. I went shopping. After I found the margarita machine for sale near where I was having lunch, I just couldn't leave it."

Maven walked over to the machine and stared at it. "Should we clean it first? Before we use it? How did you find this thing?"

"I was bored, so I was checking out Craigslist at lunch. I saw this. Answered the ad. Voila. Our parties are going to be huge. We'll put a pledge on it. In charge of serving them. I can see it now."

Chance rubbed his eyes. "No pledges. I don't want to talk about the pledges again until January 7th okay? I can't think about them at all. Vonni, which room did you choose?"

"I didn't pick a room." Was I supposed to?

Chance looked at Maven. "Where did you put her stuff?"

"Fuck. I left it in the car in the lot three blocks from here. Wasn't thinking. I'll go get it. Be right back." Maven squeezed my hand. "Sorry, Giovanna. I had my mind on other things." He winked at me. "Like pasta."

I covered my eyes with my hand and hoped my cheeks weren't as red as I thought they probably were. How could I be so fine with sleeping with all of them and then embarrassed at the innuendo? "It was really good pasta, Maven. Thanks for it."

Banyan snorted and then that turned into a full on laugh. "Oh, look how you got him all red."

Maven grabbed his coat and was out the door with a groan. Chance grinned at both of us. "So you see what I mean about this place? Good bones. Lots of work. Everything is old."

"And beautiful." I interrupted him. "Yes, it's old, but it is so beautiful. I hope you keep some of the furniture. Maybe in one of the living rooms?"

Chance reached out and stroked my cheek. "Maybe I'll do that."

"So what do we think? Margaritas? Tonight? And a movie? Sweetheart, you pick the movie."

They wanted me to pick the movie? "Did you guys like *French Kiss,* or are we thinking it's a different genre movie tonight?"

They talked about movies for a second, but I wasn't really listening. My mind had wandered, and not into a story that involved movies and a serial killer in a movie theater. No, I was staring at the margarita machine. What did it do? Blend the stuff?

"Does that taste good?"

Chance and Banyan stopped talking and turned to me. Banyan put his hand on the machine. "Sure does. You want one?"

"Maybe." I decided early on not to drink. Did that mean I had to never try it? "I told Maven tonight that I don't drink because I've seen it make my father sad. I don't need that in my life. But I have to admit I've always been curious."

Banyan rocked back on his seat. "So we'll make the movie a comedy."

Chance rolled his eyes. "Banyan."

He held up his hands. "Okay, sorry. That was stupid. I'm not that dumb. Try it. If it makes you sad, don't do it again."

"Only if you want to." Chance walked into the living room and grabbed the bags he had there. "Which room do you want? Since you didn't pick one."

I wasn't sure how to answer that. "I'm not sure which ones you guys picked. I only know which one is Maven's."

"I'm one up from him. The wallpaper is kind of black and gold. Banyan took the green room." They were all really pretty and good choices for them to have made.

"How about the one with purple on the walls? Is that taken?"

He shook his head. "You'll be on the top floor. You'll love the views. It's yours. Whenever Giovanna is here, the purple room is hers."

Banyan shrugged. "Fine by me. Who were you proclaiming that to? The universe?"

Chance groaned. "Kiss my ass. I'm putting these in your room, Vonni. I hope you like them."

He bought me something? "What is it? Thank you, by the way, for whatever it is."

"Look when you're alone. It's a surprise."

He took the stairs two at a time. Banyan nudged me with his elbow. "I'm going to clean this thing. Then you can have one."

"Do you know how to clean it?"

He scrunched up his face. "No, but I'm sure I can figure it out."

"Let's do it together."

His whole face lit up. "Awesome."

THE FACT I'd never had a margarita and had spent an hour of my afternoon scrubbing the machine wasn't lost on me. There had to be some sort of dramatic irony to that fact. I just couldn't focus on it when I was wearing gloves and up to my elbows in dish soap. A Google search had told us that the major parts were all dishwasher friendly.

I'd tried to send Banyan out to buy some dishwashing detergent. Chance's house was always ready for him, sort of. He obviously had someone else clean it and no on hand cleaning supplies, which just didn't make sense to me. What if he spilled? Did he call someone? In any case, Banyan told me they had groceries delivered and he'd gone on his app to order instead of going out to get the stuff. He hummed while he scrubbed, which I found really endearing.

I wasn't sure I knew the song, and I didn't even know if he knew that he did it. We'd gotten everything scrubbed, cleaned, and plugged in which meant it was time to put in the ingredients and see if it worked. Banyan assured Chance he had seen that it worked before he took it. I left them to the discussion and to fill up the machine with the ingredients.

Chance had brought me a present, and I still hadn't seen it. I ran the three flights of stairs to my room. I didn't really get presents. My family made donations in my name to various causes they supported.

I found the room I picked, and my suitcase was waiting. Maven had come back some time during our cleaning and headed upstairs to nap. He must have stopped to bring up my bag, which meant going a whole two staircases out of his way. I would have to thank him.

On the bed were two brown shopping bags. I opened them up, and then stopped as stunned wonder turned into giggles I couldn't control. Chance had bought me underwear. A ton of it. He'd filled two bags worth of underwear. I picked up one of the bras. He'd gotten the size right. How had he done that? I had to try all of it on, which was going to take a few minutes to do so. That was okay. With Maven asleep, no one was going to start the margaritas just yet, and I wasn't one hundred percent I wanted one.

I shut the door to the bedroom and got busy trying them on. An hour later, having quickly showered, I was in a new pair of panties and a bra beneath my jeans and t-shirt. I felt... decadent. Every single pair he had bought me fit.

My cheeks had to be pink from the state of arousal I was in just thinking about him picking out each pair, one by one. Still, I pretended all was normal. That was part of this. He wanted to know I was in them.

He didn't necessarily want me out of them yet.

I strolled into the kitchen. "Hi."

Maven was up, sitting on top of the table instead of the chairs. He'd done that in the SPiI house, too. Was that just his thing? Chance leaned against the counter, and Banyan stared at the margarita machine, which buzzed like it was on.

He looked up first. "Hey, sweetheart. What were you doing?"

"Took a shower. Got dressed again." I walked over to Chance and leaned next to him. I placed my head on his arm, and he leaned his head down on top of mine. "Thank you. Lavender."

Chance's body jumped slightly, which I could feel thanks to where I leaned on him. He cleared his throat. "Cool."

"Yep."

Maven jumped off the table. "Let's fire it up."

Banyan picked up a plastic cup. "You want to try the first one, Mave? Tell us if it's any good. Or if I need to adjust the recipe at all."

"Yep." He held out his cup. "I'll be the margarita guinea

pig. I hear you may be joining us in the evils of liquor, gorgeous?"

"So he is of course, talking to me." Chance laughed. "I mean, I'll take the compliment. Thanks. I've always wanted to be gorgeous."

Maven laughed. "Now now, Chance-y, don't get your feelings hurt. You have a pretty face, too. But this time I'm talking to that redhead leaning on you. Joining us?"

"Yes." I'd made up my mind just as he'd asked me. "If I don't like it, I won't do it again."

Maven pressed on a lever, and the small machine pressed out half a glass of margarita into Maven's waiting cup. "You know that if we use this during the parties, we're going to have a huge mess."

"That's what pledges are for." Banyan laughed, and then grimaced. "Sorry, Chance. No pledges. I know."

Chance ran a finger up my arm. "How is it, Mave?"

Maven took a long sip. "Good. You got it right. I never doubted you, Ban. No one makes a drink like you do or follows the directions to put it in the machine."

Banyan rolled his eyes. "We all have our talents. I'll pour. Move."

Maven got out of his way as Banyan poured three drinks and filled up Maven's the rest of the way. He handed me mine. "Drink it slowly. That's strong stuff even though it's sweet."

"Thanks. I might take one sip and put it down."

He nodded at me before he winked. "Whatever makes you happy. No peer pressure. Don't drink unless you want to."

"Don't listen to him." Chance sighed. "Banyan watches a lot of movies of the week."

Banyan passed out the glasses. "We have a new

member in our midst tonight, gentlemen. The lovely Giovanna is keeping us civilized this vacation from school. Thank you, sweetheart." He lifted his glass. "We always say the same thing when we toast. Here's to Carter. Wherever he is, may he say good things about all of us."

"Here, here." Chance raised his glass and then downed at least half the contents of the glass. Maven was silent but didn't drink as much in the first pull as Chance did. Banyan took a long sip and turned away before I could see how much he downed. I took a small taste. It was sweet. Was there alcohol in this?

I'd never had it, but I'd always heard it was bitter. I took another sip.

"What do you think?" Chance asked me right before he finished his drink.

"It's good." I answered him. He had gone through that fast. Was I supposed to drink it like that? "Who is Carter?"

Chance walked over to the margarita machine. "My dead roommate."

"What?" I hadn't expected that answer or the way Chance's shoulders tightened when he said it.

Maven answered me. "There were twenty-one of us in the pledge class when we started. There are twenty brothers in our year. That's because Carter died over Christmas break. Banyan was my roommate, Carter was Chance's. We were all pretty tight. Even within pledge classes, there are breakdowns of friendships."

I raised my eyebrows. "Cliques?"

"Not really, but fine, we'll use that word. It was the four of us. Pretty rough." Maven looked away and took a gulp of his margarita. "I actually might have been wrong. I don't know if there is enough tequila in this."

I hated to bring it up if they were sad, but they'd toasted Carter. "How did he die?"

"In a car accident, on an icy road on Nantucket. He was with his family. We all were, actually. But he stormed out." Chance shook his head. "Pissed at his dad. Just like that. He was gone. A lot of that in this world. Just like that and —boom—dead."

Banyan sipped his drink. "I'm thinking the time to stop toasting Carter may have been reached."

"You think?" Chance rolled his eyes. "Sorry, Vonni. I have a lot of mixed feelings about what happened that night, and I might as well leave it alone. How is your first drink?"

I stared down at it. I'd been feeling sort of jovial, but now I wasn't sure I was in the mood. "Good."

"She said that before." Banyan backed out of the room. "Come on. Movie. Comedy. Not so much for Giovanna but for you, Chance. No more toasting Carter if it's going to make you do a one-eighty in your mood."

Chance shook his head. "Going outside for air."

He stormed out of the room and slammed the front door. Maven cocked his head to the side. "You know how he gets when he's mad. I've never seen it with Carter before, but maybe there's something he's dealing with. Some kind of trigger. Don't poke at him when he's on edge. He'll be out there all night."

Banyan set down his drink. "I'll go talk to him."

"Leave him. There's nothing you can say right now that isn't going to make it worse. He needs time. Start the movie. He'll come back. Giovanna's here. He's not going to miss out on that."

I wasn't sure exactly what to do. Maven said to leave Chance out there. I supposed he knew best. Everything had been really fun and even enticing. He'd been rubbing my arm. We both knew the color of my underwear. And then it all shifted.

Sitting down on the couch with Maven and Banyan, I tried to get lost in the movie. It wasn't one I'd seen before, but it had a guy from a sitcom I liked and an actress who did a lot of slapstick. None of us laughed. I checked the clock every five minutes. Chance had been out there for half an hour. He had to be freezing. It was seriously cold.

I rose. "I have to check on him. I'll be right back."

Maven shrugged, looking at Banyan. "Anyone can turn around his night, it's her."

I went outside, foregoing my coat. Maybe my being cold might encourage him to come back inside where it was warm. I crossed my arms over my chest. Chance sat at the bottom of eight stairs. A few people passed by on the street, but he didn't move his gaze from where it landed on the sidewalk.

"You okay?"

He turned to look at me. "Vonni, it's freezing. Go back inside."

"I'll be okay for a second." I walked down toward him. "I'm worried about you."

He got to his feet. "I'm fine. I'm just... mad."

I reached the bottom, and like something out of a slow motion movie, I lost my feet. Maybe there was ice. I hadn't seen any, but it didn't matter. One second I was on my feet, and the next, I hurdled backward. Chance reached for me but missed. I hit the sidewalk on my rear end before slamming a second time into my shoulder.

I oomphed and then groaned. My rear was going to hurt, but my shoulder—it really hurt already. I had no time to fathom what happened. Chance knelt down next to me, grabbing me and pulling me to him. "Fuck. Giovanna, are you okay?"

"Think so. I don't know. My shoulder."

Chance touched my head. "You didn't hit your head right?" He felt all around it. "Where does it hurt? Your shoulder? I'm sorry."

I swallowed. Yes, the pain was real, and it was there. I hadn't made this all up in my mind. "Why are you sorry?"

"I didn't catch you."

I shook my head. "Not your fault that I fell. Not your job to catch me."

"Yes, it was." He picked me up. "How bad does it hurt? Do you need a doctor?"

I tried to think past the ever-increasing, gnawing ache. "I don't know."

"That means you need a doctor."

The door to the house opened and closed. Maven came down the stairs fast. "What happened? I heard you yell."

That was impressive, considering the noise all around us from the cars driving by. Banyan rushed outside. "Everyone okay?"

"No, Vonni fell. There's ice. Careful. I didn't catch her. I think she needs a doctor. Her shoulder."

Maven nodded. "Let's get in a cab."

That was how I managed to end my night in the emergency room. Instead of drinking margaritas.

ELEVEN

The ER buzzed with activity. Next to me, Chance couldn't sit still in his chair. He bounced his leg and shifted around constantly. Maven was on his cell phone by the doors. I wasn't sure who he was talking to, but he hadn't come over to sit with us since I'd filled out my paperwork. Banyan was still and focused on something on the ceiling.

"Why is this taking so long?" Chance asked again. Maybe it was the tenth time he voiced that question.

Banyan closed his eyes. "It won't be much longer. Maven is on it. Cool your jets."

"On what?" I'd been quiet. What was there really to say? I'd screwed up and ruined everyone's night. Tears pooled in my eyes, and I shut them. No one needed to be burdened with my emotional outbursts.

Banyan didn't answer me, so I pulled it together and lifted my lids. Once he had my gaze on his, Banyan spoke. "Pain, sweetheart?"

"Yes."

Chance put his head in his hands. "I'm so sorry."

Banyan sat forward. "You should be considering this is entirely your fault, Chance."

"What?" I wasn't sure I'd heard him right.

"It is. If he hadn't gone storming outside like that, you never would have worried about him and gone out there in the first place."

Chance nodded. "I'll take full responsibility for this. But you pissed me off, and you knew you were doing it."

"You have to talk about him, or it's going to eat you alive from the inside out."

A sharp pain rolled through me, and I hissed in a breath. They both got quiet. Chance put his hand on my leg. "Not too much longer."

I closed my eyes again. "It's not your fault I'm clumsy."

Maven came back over. "Any second."

I lifted my lids, and a few tears slipped out. I wiped them away quickly, but all three of them saw. There was nowhere for me to look that let me glance away. "I don't like hospitals. I think I'm going to die in one. In a lot of pain. Alone." Oh, the drama was moving through me now. Once I opened those floodgates, I had trouble shutting them off. I batted at my tears, but they kept coming. "And now you're all wishing you'd left me at the hotel in Pennsylvania."

"No," all three of them spoke at once.

Chance pulled my head toward him, laying it on his shoulder. "Nothing's going to happen to you here. I should have caught you."

"It was so fast. I'm sorry. I really am."

Banyan kissed my cheek. "You're going to be okay. Do you want us to call your parents?"

"No," Maven answered and then looked away. "Sorry. Ignore me. Not my decision."

I wiped at my eyes. "I haven't talked to them since they

dropped me at school. I heard from them a few times through the apps that work internationally. They put more money in my account two months ago. Then nothing. I really am afraid they got killed by poison darts."

And there I went again. Blubbering like an idiot. This time, Maven got on his knees in front of me in the hospital. "They're not dead. They're just selfish. Narcissists live forever. Only the good die young."

I snorted, and the tears stopped, but it jarred my elbow, and I ended up groaning. Just then, a man stepped in front of us. He wore a suit and a white jacket. "Maven. Good to see you. Is this the patient?"

Maven rose to his feet. "It is. Giovanna, this is my Uncle Don. He's going to take care of you and not mention to my mother that he saw me."

I nodded. "Thank you. I could have just waited."

Maven shook his head. "Maybe you could have, but I couldn't. Come on."

I got to my feet. "I'm sorry I ruined tonight, guys."

I'd started out thinking I was having one kind of day. It had taken a million stops. And now it was ending in an ER. Life was funny like that.

MY SHOULDER HAD BEEN DISLOCATED. It turned out when Maven's uncle was the doctor, you got in and out of the hospital in under an hour. I was sent back with over the counter drugs and an appointment to see his colleague for a follow up later in the week. By the time the taxi dropped us off at Chance's home, no one was talking.

I was so tired I wasn't sure I could keep my eyes open another minute. By the same token, I wasn't sure I'd be able to turn off my brain. I ached. The medicine I'd taken before leaving the hospital helped. I was sure if I could just relax, I could ignore the discomfort.

When we got to the house, Chance went into the kitchen and Banyan into the living room. Maven got a text and went up to his room to deal with it. I took the stairs slowly, ending up in what Chance had jokingly referred to as my room. I changed out of the underwear Chance had bought me and put on my flannel pajamas. I climbed into the bed.

Sex with Maven was great, dislocating my shoulder really sucked. Lots of highs and lows to the same day, it would seem.

I tried to sleep, but it wouldn't come. Instead, I grabbed my phone and sent my parents a message through the app we communicated through.

Hi there. Not sure if you are getting my messages. You haven't responded to the last two. Maybe you're busy. Just wanted to let you know that I am spending the week in New York City with friends. We had to leave campus. You might see emails about fires. I was in one, but I'm okay. I just dislocated my shoulder falling on ice, but the doctors fixed me up. Hope you are well. Merry Christmas. Love you.

If some future daughter of mine was hurt, I'd want to know.

I closed my eyes, and eventually, the day drifted away.

The bed dipped slightly, and Maven climbed into it. "Hey, don't wake up. Just missing you."

I rolled toward him, and he wrapped his arms around me. It was better that he was there. Nights didn't have to be lonely. A few moments later, or maybe it just felt that way because I dozed, the bed dipped again. Chance tucked in behind me, his hand on my side.

"This okay?"

I nodded. If Maven was okay with it, then so was I. Maven made a noise of consent, and I closed my eyes completely. Darkness was warm, and I wasn't alone in it.

Daytime came too soon, poking at my eyes, insisting I greet reality when all I wanted to do was stay right where I was, nestled between Chance and Maven. Chance muttered something, and I turned slightly to look at him. He talked in his sleep, and the last time we'd shared a room, he'd woken himself up. I snuggled against him a bit, and he settled. I closed my eyes. We didn't have to be up yet.

The next time I woke was because Maven did. He let go of me, and the movement jerked me out of my la-la land. I smiled at him, and he kissed both my eyes.

"Morning. Or should I say afternoon?" He smiled. "We did something last night after you came upstairs. How's the shoulder feeling, by the way?"

I tried to follow what he said, but I hadn't had coffee yet. "Slow down a second."

"Maven always wakes up at a million miles an hour. He's not mortal like the rest of us." Chance dug his head into the pillow. "Morning."

"You did something? Is it another margarita machine?" I'd barely gotten to drink any of the glass I'd been given.

Maven leaned up on his elbow. "We got show tickets. You liked Broadway, right? Tonight we're going out."

I sat up straight, the covers coming off me. "You did? I don't know what to say. Thank you. I'm not sure if it suffices."

Chance grinned at me. "That smile is all I needed. I cannot believe you got hurt on my steps. I..."

I touched his cheek. "Not your fault. Let's leave that where it belongs in yesterday. No bringing it in today."

Banyan stumbled into the room. He staggered a bit and then climbed into the bed next to Maven. He muttered something and dug his face into the pillow. I stared at him for a second. "Is he okay?"

Maven nodded. "Yep. He stayed up. Binge watching some kung fu thing he likes. I bet he did some damage to the margarita mix. He's just not really awake. Tends to sleep-walk when he's drunk."

Chance got out of bed. He was fully dressed. So was Maven, who had to scoot around Banyan to get out of the bed. He yawned. "See you guys downstairs. I'm ordering breakfast delivered. Speak now, or you're getting bagels and you'll be happy with it."

"Bagels are fine," Chance answered him. Neither of them were being quiet for Banyan. He didn't stir. They must be used to this.

I pointed to him on the bed. "Is he okay?"

They both nodded. "Yep. He's probably not all that drunk. Just out cold. Banyan could sleep through a bomb."

Only he hadn't. Not the night I'd woken up terrified of fire. He'd gotten up then. Plus, he'd been awake when they'd come to get me from the dorm.

I got up from the bed, and Chance bent to whisper in my ear as Maven went downstairs to order breakfast. People delivered bagels? I had that random thought before Chance's words emptied my mind of all things but him. "Blue today. I want to think of you in blue. You got hurt, so I never got to see lavender."

I leaned my head against his arm. "Do you know what you do to me when you talk like that?"

"I can imagine it's pretty similar to what happens to me when I think about it. Blue, Vonni. All day. Okay?"

I nodded. "Okay."

"Good." He tilted my chin to look at him. "Feeling okay? Are you in pain?"

"It's sore. Leave it to me to fall on the ice when you're always so good about reminding me to be careful."

He sighed. "Leave it to me to place you in that situation to fall on the ice."

I shook my head. "Would love you to stop blaming yourself for what was clearly not your fault."

Chance grinned, a piece of his brown hair falling over his eyes. I reached up and brushed it away. "I'll put on the blue."

"I'm going to spend all day hard, thinking about it."

Just then Banyan muttered something on the bed and flopped over. Chance shook his head. "He'll sleep it off and be down by dinner. Just in time to go see the show."

Chance winked at me before he left the room. I took a deep breath, my gaze traveling to Banyan. What had made him want to stay up all night watching kung fu movies and drinking margaritas? Was that just something that guys did? Or maybe girls did it, too, and it was one of those things I was out of the loop on.

I kissed him on the head, and he smiled in his sleep. I needed coffee. My phone flashed, and I walked over to it. My parents had actually responded.

Don't slip on any more ice. Merry Christmas. Happy New Year. Things here are amazing... Mom.

Well then. I supposed that was that.

Except it wasn't. I sunk down to the floor, putting my head in my hands, and I cried. As hard as I could, silently. Banyan was asleep, so he wouldn't see it. I'd been hurt, and granted, I was going to be fine. But the best they could do was to tell me not to slip on any more ice?

Anything would have been better than that. Didn't they miss me? Didn't they care?

I put my head on my knees. I was so lost in my pity party that I didn't hear Banyan get out of the bed and come over to me. He dropped down on the floor, which was when I noticed him. His arms came around me.

"Whatever it is"—his voice was low—"it'll be okay eventually. That, I can promise you. Whatever it is."

I sucked in my tears. "Sorry. I don't do this. I don't cry."

"Me neither." He laid his head on my shoulder.

"I didn't mean to wake you." I wiped my eyes. "Sorry."

He kissed the side of my face. "Say sorry one more time. That'll be three times in thirty seconds. Then you can officially stop saying it altogether. You didn't wake me. Or if you did, it's okay. How did I get up here?"

This was nice, sitting with Banyan. I'd assumed he'd be out cold all day. "You sleep walked in this morning. Maven and Chance said you do that when you're drunk."

He rubbed his eyes. "I wasn't drunk. I stayed up watching movies. Fell asleep on the couch. Maybe I just sleepwalk when you're too far away from me."

"Then you're going to be walking the streets to my dorm when we get back to school."

He stuck his bottom lip out. "I've gotten used to these past days. You can't really be going back to your dorm."

I laughed, the thought making my shoulders rock. "I can't live in a frat house."

"I suppose not." He patted my leg. "There, I made you laugh. So, why were you crying?"

I almost couldn't speak the words. "I told my parents what happened to me, and they didn't care. All pretense of giving a shit about me has fled. I'm just feeling... sorry for myself."

He didn't answer me for a second. "My parents never gave a shit. Poor little rich kid, I know. I don't have it so hard. But I know how you feel. I care that you slipped on some ice. You're in now with me. With Maven. With Chance. We'll always care."

Until they went back to school. The thought hit me hard, but I kept my face passive. There was no way this could continue, not when they were back to being SPiI brothers and I was lost in my books with whatever part time job I found.

"Thanks, Banyan. I like being in."

I didn't lie. That was going to make being out so much harder.

WE SPENT the rest of the day hanging out around Chance's house. I walked room to room with him. He'd point out how he saw each room, and I took notes on my phone. I leaned against the wall in the third bedroom when he nudged me with his shoulder. "What are you thinking?"

"A million things." There were hundreds and hundreds of stories in this place. Every room could be a different story. Maybe a woman was locked in this room for fifty years.

Chance walked over to the window. "Give me one. The most prevalent at the top of your mind."

"This is going to be your forever home, right?" I moved until I could look down through the window with him. The street was quiet. Occasionally, a car drove by. Maven had told me earlier that if I went two blocks from here the traffic would be so bad I wouldn't want to go near it.

He turned to look at me. "My forever home?"

"Maybe this is a concept that is... middle class?" My mother would able to speak on this subject better than I could. "But there's this idea that you have a home and you stay in it forever. That's home. Period. You might, I don't know, get a beach house or a cabin in the woods, but you still have that central place. Your forever home. You live and die there. Raise your kids."

Chance nodded. "I get it. I hadn't thought of it like that but, yes, this will be my forever home if I can manage it. I want to live here. I don't know if I'll have kids, but if I do, I'd raise them here."

I raised my eyebrows. "Assuming that's what your wife or husband wanted? Or partner? Whatever."

He smirked at me. "I want you, Vonni. Or did you miss that when I came in your hand? People are attracted to whatever they're attracted to, and I'm all for that. For me, that's always been female."

I shrugged. "I didn't want to assume. It could be both."

"Not so far." He drummed his fingers on the window-pane. "So you wanted to know if this is my forever home, and I said yes, and you said as long as my wife wanted it. Yes, I suppose. I mean, I hope she would want it."

He was right. A girl would have to be crazy not to want to live here. Unless she loved the country or she was richer than he was and had an even bigger place. I shrugged. This was getting off base. Assuming they'd worked that out before they got married, she wanted to live here. "I guess my only point is that she might have some decorating thoughts. Like maybe you should leave something for her to do."

"So just the basics then and let her put her touch on it when this hypothetical wife moves in here with me?"

I patted his arm. "Yes. That was it."

"Vonni, are you wearing the blue ones?"

I pulled down the side of my shirt just a bit so he could see the strap. "You asked. Of course I did."

"You might not. I mean"—he sucked in his breath—"you might pick another color to torment me just a little bit."

Oh, so this was part of the game. "Huh. Well, maybe I will. Just not today. I wore blue."

He thumbed the strap he could see. "I'm going to take you out of your panties tonight. After the show."

I leaned against him. "Sounds like a plan."

Sometimes I couldn't believe the things that came out of my mouth. I was the girl who said nothing, and I'd just said that to him. Who was I here? And could it last?

THE SHOW WAS SPECTACULAR. At one point, a character appeared in the middle of the audience out of nowhere and everyone gasped. Banyan had looked sort of bored when the show started, but even he had gotten into the music. I didn't remember the last time I laughed so hard.

Banyan took my hand in his and squeezed. He leaned over to whisper in my ear. "See? I told you that things would get better."

He'd been right, even if it was putting a Band-Aid on a gaping wound. I was happy tonight, and that would have to do.

We left the theater, and Maven jumped on his app to call a ride share car. It was a beautiful night. Brisk, but not freezing. The city seemed to glow. There were lights everywhere. "Do you guys do this all the time? Go to shows?"

Chance put his arm around me, drawing me to him. He smelled like coffee. "No. Never, actually. This is touristy. We live in Manhattan, but this isn't what we usually do."

"We didn't grow up together, but we must have encountered each other on more than one occasion and not known it," Maven finished.

"Doing what?"

Banyan shrugged. "Clubs. Bars. Parties. Lots and lots of parties. That's how we got so good at it."

"Seems like a funny thing to say. Being good at partying. Can you be bad at parties?"

They all said '*yes*' at the same time. When they agreed, they really agreed.

"Surely you guys must study. I mean, you're smart. You're headed for med school, Chance. And you want to go to law school, Maven. Banyan, you put out a tremendous amount of work. It can't be partying all the time."

The car arrived, and Banyan walked over to open the door. "I put in the minimum amount of work to maintain the required GPA. Nothing more, not ever."

Chance was right behind me. The streets of New York seemed louder all of a sudden. I couldn't say exactly why. "Imagine what you could do if you did more than what was required."

"Nothing interesting." Banyan winked at me.

I scooted into the SUV, the guys crowding in around me and behind me. Chance ended up in the back, which couldn't be comfortable. "Switch," I told him, and he and I bumped into each other until I was in the back of the car.

The driver pulled out into traffic, horns blaring. Maven turned to look at me. "Chance studies like a son-of-a-bitch. I have never found school to be all that hard to manage. I do a minimum amount of work, and I make good grades. Everyone in our fraternity has a 3.5 or better. I have better." He shrugged. "I've never thought about it, but it starts early. Even as wealthy as we were, I had to be pretty good at school to get into the best ones. Otherwise, they would have had to make some kind of large donation, and it would have been a whole thing I'd never hear the end of."

Banyan climbed into the back seat, which caused the driver to tell him to sit down. "Sorry." He gave the woman a broad smile. "I wanted to be closer to Giovanna and further from Maven and his deep thoughts."

Maven laughed, throwing his head back. "What now?"

"You guys don't have to tour me around New York. Whatever you were going to do, I could come along with you or wait behind and read. Or take myself out. Don't worry about me."

Chance shook his head. "We've got to get her a fake ID. Not so you can drink, just so you can go, Vonni. Can you make that happen, Banyan?"

He held up his phone. "On it."

"It's like whatever you want, you guys can have, isn't it? You know someone."

Chance nodded. "Sometimes. And sometimes it's like we can't have anything we want at all."

Banyan scoffed, his fingers moving faster than I could follow on his phone while he texted. "Don't know what he's talking about. I can have anything I want."

I waited for his easy, joking grin, but it didn't come. Chance stared at him, a sad gaze clouding his expression before he made eye contact with Maven, who shook his head. Chance smiled at me. "Okay, one more night staying in. Presumably, by the time we wake up tomorrow, Banyan will have procured your fake ID. And then tomorrow night, we'll go out. Oh, and I've made arrangements for New Year's."

I leaned forward. "What are we doing?"

"Yeah," Maven added. "What are we doing?"

Chance grinned at me slowly. "That's for me to know and you three to find out when I deem it appropriate."

Banyan put his phone in his lap. "Done."

I cleared my throat. "What if I didn't want a fake ID?"

Banyan leaned against the window, slightly closing his eyes. "Then you can cut it up and throw it out."

"Do you not want one," Maven asked me, capturing my gaze with his blue eyes.

I shrugged. "I guess it's fine. Next time you could ask."

Banyan shook his head. "I almost never ask." He smiled at me, opening his eyes. "But if you want me to, I can try."

"I do." It seemed important to put that out there.

TWELVE

We stopped at a restaurant and ate. It was tapas, and the food was supposed to be delicious. Banyan ordered a bottle of sparkling wine from California.

"For a bottle of sparkling wine to be labeled champagne, it has to be made in Champagne, France and produced using the méthode champenoise." Banyan took a sip of his drink. The waiter had poured me some without blinking. It probably had something to do with the money Maven slipped him when we sat down. Or maybe they just didn't care here.

Chance kicked me under the table lightly. "Banyan likes to think he knows everything about wine."

"I do. I was practically breast fed on the stuff." He shifted in his seat. "I'm going to paint tonight. I'm getting jittery."

Maven slammed down his phone. "My uncle didn't keep his promise. My mom knows I'm in town."

"How pissed is Barbara?" Chance wiped his face. "And when should we expect her?"

Maven put his head in his hands. "Tomorrow. Actually,

I'd really love to keep her from the house. Once she comes in, she never gets out. And she'll spit her vile nonsense at all of you."

She sounded absolutely horrifying. My parents talked badly about people but not to their faces. I wasn't exactly sure which was worse. "I'm sorry. This is on me. You wouldn't have called him if not for me."

"Not your fault. You hardly fell on purpose." He raised one dark eyebrow. "Want to help me out?"

I supposed I would, since Maven had a way of getting people around him to do what he wanted. "Sure."

"Careful agreeing to that so quickly. We don't know what he wants yet. And when it comes to Barbara, he's not reasonable. Anything to get away from Mommy." Banyan looked at his menu. "What do we all want to eat?"

Next to me, Chance had gone still. He put a hand on my thigh, squeezing it gently. "What do you want her to do, Mave?"

Maven shrugged. "Be my girlfriend."

Chance's hand dug into my thigh for a second before he quickly eased up. "Come again?"

I opened my mouth. "I thought none of you wanted girl-friends."

Banyan set down his menu. "That's not going to work for me."

Maven held up his hands. "For two hours. Be my girl-friend over lunch with my mother. She'll love you. You're all kinds of interesting, and you'll get her off my ass for a while. She'll go back to her own world after. Couple of hours."

I swallowed. "I'm not great in those situations. I realize I've been chatty with all of you, but I'll probably freeze and be very, very quiet."

He nodded. "That's fine. She'll interrogate you and talk a lot. You'll hardly have to do anything."

"Maybe she doesn't want to, and you've just put her on the spot." Chance leveled a glance to Maven. "I'll go. She can poke at me for hours. I won't mind it."

Maven tilted his head to the side. "She knows you. Giovanna will be new. What do you say? Fine to tell me no."

I was going to do it. How bad could it really be? "You and that superpower."

His smile was broad. "Awesome."

Banyan drummed his fingers on the table. "Can we order?"

I looked down at the menu. *Be my girlfriend....*

For just a second, my heart had stuttered. I didn't mind the sound of that. But it wasn't just Maven I wanted to hear it from. Chance's hand was still on my leg and across the table. Banyan grinned at something Maven said, which lit up the table. I was in big trouble. They'd never ask me to pick. They'd all been very clear they weren't boyfriend material. I was going to have to keep my heart intact. For the first time I realized they had the ability to break it.

Yes, friendship was how this had to stay. I could never let myself even imagine anything else. I couldn't have them all.

How on earth would I ever choose?

I shook my head. What did it matter? We were friends and they were showing me a good time for a little while. The vacation from myself. That's all it would be.

WE HAD all stayed up to watch an old black and white

movie in the second living room, but only Chance and I were actually still awake. Banyan snored across the room. His head was in a funny position. I bet if I moved him slightly, he'd stop. Not that it mattered. Maven was out cold in a lounge chair, one arm flung over his head, his mouth slightly open.

The movie ended, and Chance elbowed me. "Come on. My room." I took his hand and let him lead me to the end of the hallway. "I think your bed might be more comfortable. I had a bunch of mattresses brought in when I took over the place. They should all be the same, and yet, they're not." He gave me a dramatic sigh. "I want you to myself. Tonight. Is that okay?"

I nodded. I'd craved this all day. "Yes."

Chance shut the door and locked it. "It opens from the inside. You want out, you just turn the lock and go."

I walked over to him and put my hands on his shirt, grabbing on to the white cotton. "I'm not worried. You don't have to be."

"I'm always going to want to make sure you're okay." He nuzzled his nose in my hair. "I know this is... different. Like how we've become friends is not exactly the status quo."

I nodded. "A little unconventional to say the least. But you guys do this, right? You share girls. That's what you told me."

He sighed, his hand coming into my hair. "Not like this, no. It's not usually this long term."

I digested that piece of information. Chance kissed my temple, and I wanted to get lost in the moment. Still, I had to know. "I never want to be where I'm not welcome. I've spent most of my life as the third wheel with people who made me but didn't seem to want me around. Am I over-staying my welcome?"

He jolted, his arms coming around me. "Are you kidding? No, this isn't me saying to go. This is me saying to stay. Even though this is so different."

I kissed him, wanting my lips pressed to his. He sighed against me and then took over the kiss. Chance whispered my name before he laid me down on the bed. "You wore the blue all day."

He slipped my sweater off me and stared down at my breasts, confirming for himself what he'd just said. "I spent hours in several lingerie departments. I'm afraid that the women there probably know about my little obsession."

"Well, then they're just jealous." I loved feeling this way with him. Chance made me feel... sexy in a way I didn't usually. As though his eyes couldn't stop looking at me. "That I got to wear all the beautiful stuff. How did you know my size?"

He gave me a sideways smile. "I looked. At your bra. I wish I could say I had some magic ability to tell women's bra sizes, but I don't. I wanted to know, so I found out."

I nodded. "Pragmatic."

"I tend to be."

We quit talking. The only sound in the room was the small moans Chance made when he kissed me, again and again. His finger strummed up and down the strap of the bra, stopping before he got down to my breasts, never actually touching them. He lifted his gaze to meet mine for a second. I nodded at him. Yes, he could touch me.

He undid my bra, setting it aside before he clasped my nipple in his mouth and bit down, hard. I cried out, digging my nails into his back. He sucked on one nipple, sending jolts of pleasure through my body as he reached with his other hand to massage the other.

My breasts weren't usually all that sensitive, but when

Chance touched them, it was an entirely different thing. I trembled with pleasure, my back slightly arching off the bed. "Fuck, Chance."

He stopped sucking to smile at me. I pushed on him to turn him over. This couldn't be just about me. I wanted to touch him, to know his body, too. I pulled his shirt off of him, more clumsily than he'd done for me, and bent over to kiss him right above his heart.

Chance touched my cheek, stroking his thumb down the side of it. "You're so pretty. You know that, right?"

I put my finger on his mouth to stop him, and he bit the end of it. In this position, it was easy to rub against him, even with our clothes on. He was hard, and each time I pushed on him, he'd moan. I loved the sound. It wasn't going to be enough, not right then. We needed our pants off, and he must have known it, too.

We scrambled to strip off the rest of our clothes in an almost frenzied manner. Then his mouth was on mine again, fast and hot. Chance sighed. "Slow down," he whispered. "We've got nothing to rush to."

I tried to. He was right. Chance flipped me over, and we lay side-by-side instead of me on top of him.

This wasn't a race and getting finished sooner wasn't necessarily the goal. Instead, we lay on the bed together, touching and stroking. The longer we touched, the harder he got, and I wasn't even caressing his cock yet.

Eventually, I couldn't resist him anymore. My ears rang from wanting him and there wasn't another second I could delay the outcome before I was just going to lose my mind. I squirmed, trying to get closer and he smiled against my mouth. He liked this, the little bit of torturing me, of the delayed gratification.

I stroked the top of his erection, and he closed his eyes.

His cock jumped in my hand. He might be good at holding off but that didn't mean he didn't want to come, too. He sucked in a long breath. "Better grab the condom while I still can."

He rolled away from me and opened the drawer in the side table next to the bed. A few seconds later he had sheathed himself. His cock stood out, erect and tempting.

My insides pulsed. He slipped a finger inside of me and found my clit with his thumb. I forced my eyes to stay open, just for a few extra seconds. I wanted to see him doing this to me, I wanted to know I had his total attention. For those few moments before I had to close my eyes in order to just feel how he played my body like an instrument, I could see something in his gaze I couldn't name. What was it?

Whatever it was passed fast and soon I had to let my lids close. I had to just be in that moment, just feel what he did to me. He pressed hard, and I shuddered. My breaths came in quick gasps. I wasn't going to be long. He'd revved me up with all of the petting.

I opened my eyes. "I want to come with you inside of me."

"Let's do it." He pulled me beneath him. "This way. So your arm doesn't hurt."

I beamed down at him. "That's right. I somewhat remember this." I arched my back to slip him inside of me. He was big and he stretched me.

"Fuck, Vonni, you feel good. How do you feel this good?" He kept himself above me. "Like... fuck. I don't know."

I couldn't even begin to analyze how perfect he fit inside of me. Chance moved his hips, hitting me in all the right places, and I cried out. Yes, he'd just managed to rub against my clit and that was exactly what I needed. What I always craved.

In and out we rubbed and stretched until I was begging and he was crying out my name. Still, neither of us had come. Chance had wanted this to last, and he was getting his wish. Fuck. Why couldn't I come? I needed to come. I needed to right then. Fuck. What I needed was Chance. I needed... I needed...

He jerked his hips, hitting my clit really hard, and I exploded. The world whited around my eyes. He said my name on a whisper, exploding inside of me.

This was... everything.

I OPENED my eyes when the morning light blasted through the windows in the room. I didn't remember falling asleep. I really must have passed out. Chance had an arm around me, and I slept on top of his other arm. He breathed deeply, evenly. We were both totally naked.

He said something, but it was a mumble, and he wasn't awake. The last thing I remembered was... yeah... coming hard. I rubbed at my eyes. I hoped I hadn't passed out.

A knock sounded on the door. "Hey, sorry to disturb, but it's almost lunch. I need Giovanna to get up. Get dressed. Get ready for my mother."

Chance groaned. "Fuck. Me."

I rolled over in his arms. "We don't really get to sleep in, do we?"

He smiled, a long lazy grin. "No, but I slept great. Did you?"

"Ah, yes." Should I tell him the truth? "I don't actually remember falling asleep."

He rubbed the back of my head before he kissed me. "Oh you were so cute. Curled right up and fell asleep in my arms. I wore you out. That's all."

The knock came again. "Did you guys wake up?"

"Maven is relentless when he's anxious." He rolled over. "Yes, we're up." Chance got out of the bed. He grabbed his boxers and pulled them on before he flung open the door. "Morning, Maven. Did you say something about lunch with your mom? Because I couldn't hear you obsessing about it down the hall or anything."

As he strode into the room, Maven laughed. "Just wanted to make sure that Giovanna had enough time to get ready."

What kind of thing did I have to get ready to do? "I can shower. Is there anything else I have to do?"

Just then, Banyan appeared holding a black bag. "It dawned on me that you don't have the right clothes. Not to eat with Barbara. I ordered some. Try them on, I got multiple sizes just to be careful."

The blankets were on top of me, and I pulled my knees to my chest. I hadn't thought about clothes at all. I guessed that mattered? "Is she going to judge me on my clothes?"

Banyan plopped down on the bed. "Yes. Maven's mom is not nice. She's smart, good at her job, and she works hard. But she can be condescending as hell."

Maven shrugged. "Pretty good description. Want to back out?"

I did. But I wouldn't. "I know that you've all seen me naked at this point." I couldn't believe I uttered those words, but I did. "I'd still like to get out of bed unviewed, if that's possible."

Chance rocked back on his feet. "Let's give her a few minutes."

"Thanks for thinking of the clothes, Banyan."

He winked at me as he exited. Maven stayed behind as the other two left. "I won't let her make you upset. It should just be lunch and then done. If she gets... nasty with me, that's fine. But if she says anything to you that you don't like, we're out. Okay?"

I shook my head. "Is she going to just go around saying obnoxious things?"

"No. She'll say it so that you're not one hundred percent sure you were at all insulted. It'll be beautifully delivered. And then she'll change the subject. Forget it. Don't go. You don't need this."

I shook my head. "Give me a minute. I'll get ready."

If there was anything my years of trailing after my parents as their third silent wheel taught me, it was how to get through uncomfortable situations unscathed. Maven nodded. "You're really the best."

He turned and practically fled the room. Most people would never see Maven like this. I shouldn't be so sure of that, but I was. Chance had called it right. When Maven was anxious, he obsessed. If I could somehow make this whole thing less stressful for him, then that was what I was going to do.

I ENDED up wearing the clothes that Banyan bought me. They weren't fancy, but he had decided to put me all in black. I had on a pair of black pants and a sleeveless black tank top that had ruffles near the top. He'd topped it with a blazer that was a shade lighter black than the rest of the outfit. He'd also thought to get me some black boots.

If I ever had to blend into the night like some sort of spy,

I'd be golden. I could picture it now. I was hiding in a back alley and...

No. Internally, I shook my head. I had to stay present. In the here and now. Barbara Stone wasn't to be trifled with. That much I discerned as soon as we sat down in the small French bistro around the corner from where Chance lived. She'd ordered a scotch, even though it was noon, and hadn't touched it yet.

I sipped my water.

"So let me get this straight, most of the time you lived in Kenya?"

Maven hadn't touched his food. He'd ordered a *croque monsieur,* and he was playing with it, not really eating. I'd stuck with salad. It was easier to move around on the plate. "Yes. That's right. My mom was always particularly interested in warfare, as it changes from culture to culture. There is evidence of ancient mass murder in Kenya. It was a good place for her to start."

She set down her fork. "And you just hung around?"

"I was homeschooled. I studied. A lot." *Read books that no one approved of.*

Barbara was a beautiful woman. I'd thought she would be flawless, fixed up by plastic surgeons to look her son's age, but that wasn't the case. She had lines by her eyes and mouth. If I recalled correctly, she was an attorney. Maybe aging was something she'd actually had to do to gain credibility in court.

"It's just fascinating. Very different from his upbringing. We stayed around here most of the time except for vacations, and I'm afraid it was a bit of a mundane existence. Skiing. Yachts. I'm not sure Maven would know what to do with himself without luxury around."

He shifted in his seat, and I sat back in mine. "Everybody wants to be comfortable if they can be. But Maven stayed back at school, and would still be there if he were allowed, to do community service over his whole vacation. He rescued me from a fire. I'm pretty sure he can handle himself in most situations."

I might have made that seem more dramatic than it was, and I didn't care. He stared at me over his glass of red wine. Unlike his mother, he was touching his drink. "Thanks."

"She likes you." His mother smirked. "But then, who wouldn't like you? Did he buy you those thousand dollar boots? He does like to spend on his women."

I almost choked on my water. Thousand dollar boots? I had been walking around on a grand worth of shoes. What had they done to the boots? Was it the cow that the leather came from that was worth so much money?

"I think there are lots of women who wouldn't like me." He smiled at her. "With Dad being a felon, after all. I mean we pretend he's not, right? But he is. Such a fun word. Felon."

His mother shot him daggers for a second and then took a long pull from her scotch glass. "Your father is fine. He is rehabbing very nicely. Seeing the prison psychiatrist. You could visit him when next I go."

"I didn't ask how he was, and I'm good without seeing him." He set down his fork and pushed away his plate. "He didn't have time for me when he was out of prison, and I don't have time for him now. Was there anything else? Why are we having lunch? Were you just pissed I didn't tell you I was in Manhattan? If I had, would you have left me alone?"

She smiled like he hadn't insulted her. "Why, Maven, I'm just trying to get to know your girlfriend."

He put his arm around the back of my chair. "Well, Mom. This is Giovanna. She's lovely. Smart. Kind. She's funny, but she doesn't think she is. She loves music. Movies. She lights up a room when she smiles. Totally unpretentious, and I think she's smarter than I am. She speaks her mind. And I love her red hair. Was there anything else?"

Just then, the door to the restaurant opened, and much as it shocked me, Banyan strode in like he owned the place. He was dressed differently than he'd been when we left. He'd put on a suit, and it looked like he'd been born to wear it. Actually, Maven was similarly attired. Both of them had gone for light blue. Banyan wore a tie, and Maven didn't.

He waltzed past the hostess with a smile and slid into the booth next to Barbara. "Hello, friends."

Maven's mother sat up straight. "Banyan. How nice to see you. This is a surprise."

"Well, when I heard you were having lunch with Maven and Giovanna, I had to drop by. I can't miss the chance to see my favorite of my friend's moms if I get the chance." He put his arm around Barbara, and she turned red. I looked at Maven, who smirked at Banyan before he covered the look.

Maven pointed to the food on the table. "Hungry?"

"No. Barbara, tell me, how do you do it? I've always wondered. You manage somehow to keep a thriving career, handle the stresses your husband thrust on the family, run your charities, and stay out of the gossip columns." He shook his head. "My mother has a meltdown if the store is out of her favorite coffee flavor."

Barbara pushed gently on Banyan. "Oh, stop that. The things your friend says, Maven. He's flirting with me."

Maven didn't comment but took a bite out of his sandwich. Barbara was now laughing at something Banyan said. I turned to Maven slightly. "I'm... I'm not coming up with the word I want to use."

"I'll just go with grateful. He did this for you. He'd leave me here with her on my own if he had his choice. We tend to stay out of each other's parental situations if we can. Nothing much to be done most of the time." He pointed to my salad. "Try to eat while she's distracted. I know it can be hard to when she's got that laser-sharp, judgmental eye trained right at you. Hard to chew and swallow."

I touched his arm. "I meant what I said. You'd do great anywhere you went. I don't think there's much that could intimidate you. Outside of the person across from us."

He touched the end of my hair. "Thank you. I really have come to like how you see me." He took another bite. "Make her the bad guy in a future novel."

She laughed again, and Banyan made eye contact with Maven. Something unspoken passed between them. I suspected it was thank you.

THIRTEEN

"Thanks for doing that." Maven put his arm around me as we walked down the street.

I side-eyed him. "I didn't really get to do anything. I think Banyan is the reason it didn't explode."

"You stood up for me." He kissed my cheek and then stopped me from walking to kiss me on the lips, hard. "I don't need anyone to do that. But, I liked how you did just the same."

Banyan came up behind us, pulling my hand gently. "She's coming with me. Alone. That's the price I'm exacting for having flirted with your mother for an hour and a half. Go home and hang out with Chase."

Maven let go of my hand. "Assuming she wants to go with you."

"I'm really up for anything." I looked between them. At lunch, I'd felt like they were speaking without words, and now I couldn't get over that sensation. Were there still undertones I wasn't understanding?

My lunch date nodded. "Then I'll see you two later. Did you get it?"

"It?" It took me a second to realize that he wasn't talking to me, but to Banyan.

He held out a card. "I did. Giovanna, congratulations, you're now twenty-two years old. Hold onto this. Don't get it mixed up with your real ID. Like don't try to use it to get on a plane. The bouncers won't really care to analyze it that much; you're a hot girl. TSA might feel quite differently."

I stared at the ID he handed me. "Where did you get this picture? Is that my picture that's on my library card?"

He shrugged. "It's on the school website. I downloaded. Uploaded. Boom. The guy I know made the ID. Problem?"

"No." I shook my head. "It's fine. I guess the concept of a fake ID was one thing. Having one is another."

He held out his hand. "I'll take it back."

"I need it? To go wherever you want to go the rest of the week?"

Banyan took my arm to move me out of the way of two people hurrying down the street. "Maybe. I don't know. It'll be useful for you at school if you want to go out somewhere off campus, like a bar. Up to you."

I put it in my pocket. "I'll keep it. But if I get arrested, you have to come get me out of jail. My parents are in India. I don't think they'd fly home. I'd have to stay behind bars."

Banyan's face fell. "I'd never let anything happen to you. And I'll always show up."

Maven patted Banyan on the arm and leaned over to kiss my cheek. "See you two later."

Banyan hailed a taxi, which stopped quickly for us.

"Do you guys ever take the subway?"

He shook his head. "No. I mean, I have. There was a period of time when I did it all the time just to tick off my mom because she hates the subway, but generally speaking, if I can get a car, I get one." He gave the driver an address I didn't know, and we were off, traveling, I thought, down-town and in the opposite direction of Chase's house.

"Where are we going?" The fake ID burned a hole in my pocket. Or at least it did in my imagination.

He leaned back in the seat. "I bought something a year ago. I wanted you to see it. I'd like your opinion. I haven't shown anyone yet so... you're the first. Is that okay?"

"Yes." I stared at his hard profile. Banyan had a lot of layers. He could go from easy going and funny to very serious in no time flat. Did his moods shift like that, or was he always covering one for the other?

Banyan took my hand. "Thanks. Seriously, by the way, if I have to flirt with Maven's mom one more time, I am going to lose my mind. This would be the third time." He winced. "She grabbed my leg under the table. That's why I said no more after the last time. Paying her attention to get her sharp focus off Maven is one thing. Having her basically proposition me nonverbally is something else entirely."

I scrunched up my nose. "Have you told Maven that she does that?"

"Fuck, no. Things are complicated enough in that mess of a relationship. I mean, he has to see how she responds, and that's far enough. I won't be taking her up on her propo-sition, but I think I've got to stay away from this point on."

I leaned my head down on his shoulder, deciding not to analyze why I wanted to do that after hearing about another woman hitting on him. This was all going to get muddled if I didn't get my head straightened out. "Thanks for showing up. She hadn't really done anything yet, but I could feel it coming."

"Yep. Passive aggressive bullshit."

The car slowed down, and he got out of the car, taking my hand to help me out of it. I didn't really have issues getting in and out of cars, but I'd gotten sort of used to the guys doing it regularly now. I was going to miss it when it stopped.

I squinted in the sun, looking around the block. "Where are we?"

He pointed at the building to our left. It was red brick and taller than Chance's home. "My loft. I bought a space. I'm going to paint here. This is where I'm going to do all my work."

We walked into the building together after he used his key to get through the front door. It was quiet inside, except for a buzzing from a fluorescent light. "They have this lighting all over the building. I'm going to change it in my loft. I want soft tones and natural light. Not this crap."

The elevator was slow, and it groaned before it shuddered. I didn't really consider myself claustrophobic, and I'd never been nervous in an elevator before, but I didn't like this one. Not at all.

But Banyan had a huge smile on his face. He was so happy to be in the elevator and the deathtrap skidded to a stop with a moan and a jiggle. The door opened with another key, and we stepped inside.

It was one big room with huge windows that stretched from ceiling to the floor. He left the lights off, which I appreciated, because I could really see how the room glowed from the sun coming in through the panes.

"When I saw this place, I couldn't believe it." He did a circle around the room. "I can see the canvases. I had to have it."

Banyan's grin was infectious, and soon I was beaming back. "This is a great space. Will you live here, too?"

"Yes, technically, I think this will be my home. I might crash at Chance's a lot. But this will be my home address."

I walked over to the window and looked down. The buildings were taller on this side of town. Everything looked a little bit newer. I smirked. Except for Banyan's elevator. "How long have you had it?"

"I got it over Thanksgiving. My mother checked herself into a clinic for her latest disorder, whatever it is this time, and didn't show up for dinner. I bought this the next day."

I turned around. "Congratulations, Banyan. I love it. I think you'll make great art here."

He rushed at me, picking me up by the waist and spinning me in a circle. All of this twisting was going to make me dizzy, but I just decided to go for it. I squealed, a pretty unusual noise for me to make.

I wasn't really a squealer.

Banyan set me down, bringing me against him in a hug. He smelled like sugar. I breathed him in. "Why do you smell so sweet?"

"Can't help it. My natural scent. I'm just irresistible. Like candy or donuts."

I groaned. "Seriously."

"I'm being totally serious. You had fun last night? At the Broadway show? I want to take you to my favorite dance club tonight. It could be a little intense. Nothing will happen to you as long as you're with me."

Whatever he wanted. "I'm game. Particularly with my new card that could get me arrested."

"I keep thinking..." He shook his head. "Never mind. Can I kiss you?"

I raised my eyebrows. "You think you have to ask?"

He raised his gaze slowly, his attention never moving from my eyes. "I just want to be sure. Do you suppose we could have met in a different way? Like, if Maven hadn't gotten your attention on the street that day and I'd driven up. Would we have met?"

I blinked. He'd certainly moved on from kissing me to a different subject very quickly. "You're doing the covers for the literary magazine. Maybe we would have met?"

Probably not, because I would have figured out how to manage the whole thing online and never have to meet in person, but I'd leave that as a *maybe* just for the heck of it.

He lowered his eyes, his gaze on my mouth. "I like that idea. Sure. We'll go with that."

Finally, he kissed me. His lips were soft, and we just stood there, breathing together, our lips hardly touching. And then he deepened it.

His arms came around me, and my body was on fire. Banyan had the ability to move me, and I couldn't exactly pinpoint why. Right then, I didn't even want to try. I just wanted to exist in this space in the universe where Banyan kissed me and nothing else mattered.

I pressed my tongue into his mouth, taking control for a second, and he moaned. His body hardened against my own.

"Fuck, sweetheart, we've got no furniture. It's not going to be comfortable for me to do all the things I want to do with you here."

I gave him a little shrug. "Who needs comfort?"

He raised his eyebrows. "Where do you want me?"

I pointed at the floor. "On your back. There."

He backed up, letting me go. "All right. Apparently I take directions pretty well when you're the one giving them to me."

When he was flat on his back, I straddled him, pressing my most sensitive area against his. He sucked in his breath, and I grabbed onto his shirt. "Terrible? Like too rough on the floor?"

"Sweetheart, all I'm feeling right now is your hot little body on top of mine."

I liked that answer, and so I pressed down on him and backed off, simulating what I would do to him naked, shortly. I reached down to cup the top of his cock through his pants. He sucked in a long breath. I let go and he exhaled.

"Do you want me to go down on you?" I couldn't believe how I was talking but with Banyan it felt natural. I opened my mouth and that was what came out of it. He seemed to like it. Banyan wasn't shy. He'd tell me if he wasn't okay.

He smirked. "So much. But not now, okay? Later. I want this to end in a very specific way and your mouth on me will put me over the edge."

I pouted, sticking out my lower lip. "You promised another time."

"I'll never say no to it again."

I took off all of my clothes, letting him watch my every movement. Most of the time I didn't feel sexy, ever. But I did right then. His gaze on me made me this person—this loving-being-naked-with-him-watching person.

He visibly swallowed before he took off his own attire. His penis, long and hardened, caught my attention and I walked over to stroke him, one strong movement of my hand from his balls to his tip. He visibly trembled.

"Do you have a condom?" I whispered my question. If he didn't, we were going to revisit the whole giving him a blow job scenario. No way was this just ending now.

Banyan nodded, a piece of his dark hair falling on his face. "In my pocket. I mean, I hope that's not presumptuous. I was actually not thinking that I was going to have sex on this floor. I thought maybe later? And, okay, I'm rambling." He held out his hand. "Come here, sweetheart."

I walked toward him, kneeling down to crawl up his body, hitting his cock with my breasts. He sighed. "They are soft."

I kissed his chin, his mouth, his shoulders. He smelled amazing, like cinnamon. He grabbed the condom from his pants and put himself in it. Scooting down, I stroked him one more time before I pushed myself down on him, fitting himself inside of me before I pushed down. We both groaned. Hell, this felt so good. It should be illegal.

We moved like that, neither of us speaking, not needing to. Sometimes words were in the way. I threw my head back and he grabbed onto my hands, holding onto me, and whether he meant it to be an additional connection between us or not, that was what he gave me. I stared down at him.

His gaze heated me further. Sometimes Banyan could look so serious. This was one of those moments. I felt like his canvas, as though he painted me with his eyes. I sped up my movements and squeezed my hips. I wanted him as deep as I could have him and to rub me right where I needed it. He took silent direction well. Banyan thrust hard, again and then again.

I grabbed onto my own breasts, squeezing them, and he moaned, loudly.

He liked that? I'd do it anytime. I'd never wanted anything as much as I wanted Banyan to get off. He reached between us, touching my clit, rubbing it. I ground against him, my knees pressing into the floor. Fuck, yes. I needed that. I always did.

I shouted my release, my orgasm taking me by surprise. One second I wasn't near coming and then the next I suddenly was. My own must have called his. He spent himself inside of me, a long moan. I closed my eyes.

Somewhere in the back of my mind, a thought intruded on my bliss.

How on earth was I ever going to live without this?

BACK AT CHANCE'S HOUSE, I stared at myself in a full-length mirror. Maven had joined the other two in purchasing me clothes. They had been on my bed when I returned. Now, showered and rested, I stared at myself in the outfit I was going to wear to the club I needed the fake ID for. I'd never have picked a gold dress for myself.

Still, it worked. It was strapless, and I glittered when I moved. Maven had left me a note on the dress that just said, "I want people to look at you."

I touched my neck. For some reason, in this dress, my neck looked long. The short gold number stopped right above my knees and made them look longer, too. I'd officially think of this as the looking longer dress from now on.

A knock sounded on the door. When I said come in, Chance opened it then leaned against the side of the entranceway.

He didn't smile. "That dress. I'm not sure if I want you to be in it all night or if I want you out of it immediately."

I touched the strap. "No bra in this one." I looked at his reflection in the mirror. "Can you tell?"

"Hmm." He stepped into the room. "I'm starting to think you like torturing me. You have a funny look on your face. I'm not sure you're happy."

I shrugged. "I'm not sure this dress is me. I mean, I've

kind of been on vacation from myself this week. But this might be more than I can manage."

He ran a finger down the side of my arm, and I shivered. "It's one version of you. If you don't like it for tonight, don't do it. This is, and always will be, about what you want. We're on vacation from us, too."

That was an interesting thought. He was more casual than I was. He was in a black pair of pants and a white collared t-shirt that he'd rolled up at the sleeves. I guessed he wasn't concerned with being cold. For that matter, I had to figure out how I was going to not freeze as well.

I sighed. Getting dressed up was complicated. It was just easier to stay casual. I'd never wanted to be a princess from a Disney movie. This had to be officially the last time they dressed me up like a doll.

I touched his shirt. "Who are you when you're not on vacation from yourself?"

Chance shrugged. "Pre-med student at a really good liberal arts college. Rich kid whose father beat him a lot. Motherless child. Pledge master of my fraternity. Pretty bad boyfriend. Bored. Uninterested. Seen it all. Spoiled."

Those were not the words I would have used to describe him. "Not one adjective or descriptive phrase you just used fits you. Why is it that we can understand things so well except we can never really get ourselves correctly?"

He bent over to press our foreheads together. "Maybe we do, Vonni. Maybe this really is just as you described it. Maybe this is some kind of pause from life, from ourselves. Then we all go back to who we were before Christmas Eve."

I breathed in a long, slow inhale. "Then I'll always be glad we had a couple of weeks together. And I'll miss you."

He shook his head pulling back a bit. "I didn't mean

that I was going anywhere. I'm not going to vanish just because we're back at school."

"Maybe I will." Returning to the girl without much to say.

Maven poked his head in the room. "Hey, that gold dress really works on you. I knew it would."

Chance moved toward the door. "It's dressy. You know everyone wears expensive clothes that look casual when they cost a fortune to buy." He pulled at his shirt. "Example."

I grinned at Chance. Like Banyan and Maven, he could move through moods faster than anyone I knew. Was it something about guys from New York, SPiI brothers, or the very wealthy? I might never know the answer to that question.

I stared at Maven. "Why get me more dressed up than everyone else? You don't want me to fit in?"

He put his arm around me. "I want everyone's eyes on you tonight, Giovanna."

"Okay, this is the last time you guys buy me clothes, okay? If I need something, you tell me what it is and I'll take care of it."

Maven held up his hands like I'd pointed a gun at him. "Okay, we surrender. No more spoiling Giovanna. We get it. You do look fantastic."

"Thank you. Where's Banyan? Let's take a picture."

He came through the door right at that moment. "I'm here."

All three of them were dressed very similarly. I was sure there was a difference in brands, but to my untrained eye, I couldn't see it. I stood in the middle of them, all three of them slightly behind me, and waited while Banyan used my phone to take a picture of us. One didn't do; he took four of them, and then texted it to himself and the other two at the same time.

"There. Now we're in a group chat"—he handed me back my phone—"that started with a picture of the four of us together."

Chance smirked. "Be careful. Banyan likes to group text. You'll get hundreds of messages now. About asinine things like ice cream."

Maven laughed, and Banyan groaned. It was the latter who spoke. "I was drunk. Very, very drunk. Or I'd never have texted you at two in the morning about strawberry ice cream on a night before an exam. I don't even remember doing that."

Chance put his arm around me. "I was awake, still studying, or he'd be standing here dead right now."

"You can't stand places dead, Chance." Banyan rolled his eyes. "Unless you're a zombie. Am I a zombie in this scenario?"

Maven shrugged. "Could be a vampire."

I tried to imagine what the night was going to be like. Maven dressed me in this gold dress that I was told was going to be too fancy. Should that bother me? I couldn't bring myself to care one way or the other about it. Clothing mattered little to me when it came down to it. But New York City nightclubs featured in books all the time, particularly romance novels. Couples were always meeting there and having drunken sex they couldn't remember the next morning.

Then sometimes there were unplanned pregnancies that eventually led to happily ever afters. We'd taken precautions. I wasn't going to get pregnant that evening.

Banyan handed me a black men's blazer. "It'll do for a coat. We won't be outside long."

"Don't we have to get in some kind of line?"

Maven kissed my cheek. "Not when you're with us, honey."

———————

WHATEVER I'D BEEN THINKING the club was going to be like, I'd been wrong. There were women dancing in cages above our heads. The music was loud, there was the faintest smell of something I couldn't identify but came across as musky in the air, and a lot of people staring at each other and at us.

I held onto my phone like it was a lifeline and handed my fake ID back to Banyan who had shown it to the bouncer for me on the way in. One of the ten bouncers.

Maven had been right. Everyone stared at me.

Most of the women wore white or black, the latter being more prevalent. It seemed like the ladies in white really wanted to be notice. What did they think of me in gold? I shook my hair. If they were fictional characters, I'd care because it would speak to their motivations and inner conflict. As it was, these strangers would vanish from my life and I'd never even be in a room with them again. Or if I was, I'd be clueless about it.

Maven nudged me. "You okay?"

We sat down at a table where Banyan ordered alcohol for all of us. Bottles of something or another. Whatever it was, the waiter grinned slightly when he walked away. The dance floor was crowded, and I watched people being bumped into each other in different degrees of happiness or annoyance.

"Yes." I smiled at him. "So this is what you guys do? Regularly?"

"What do you think?" Chance answered me instead of Banyan.

I stared at the place one more time. "I don't think anything. Probably not my scene. Not even in this time out from myself I'm taking."

Banyan stood. "Then let's go. I'm bored."

He was? "We just got here."

"This isn't how I want to spend the remainder of the time I have on this vacation, and I don't think they do either." He looked at Maven and Chance. "I forgot. Sometimes I hate this shit. Tonight is one of those times."

He threw money down on the table.

That was how I ended up in my gold dress, eating cupcakes from a vending machine that distributed them, drinking coffee at midnight with three SPiI brothers on a street in Manhattan. I couldn't help but smile. I liked the cupcakes a lot more than the club.

FOURTEEN

I woke up on the 31st at four in the afternoon. I was pressed between Banyan and Maven. Chance had been dragged out the night before by a high school friend, and he'd gone to hang out for a while, complaining his whole way out the door.

He hadn't been back when we'd fallen asleep.

I'd always thought of myself as a morning person, but these late nights were starting to alter my body rhythms. I yawned, and Maven groaned.

"I feel like we've been asleep a long time. Like if I move, my muscles are going to complain," he whined and winced when he rolled over.

Banyan sighed. "I was having the best dream. Had to do with popsicles. Do you remember Toasted Almonds? I really loved those."

I side-eyed him. "You dream about food? And do Toasted Almonds count as popsicles? Isn't that more like ice cream?"

"You are way too clear headed for this early in the

morning." Banyan yawned. "It was a dream. They can be popsicles."

Chance strolled into the room. "I was the one out last night, home at the butt crack of dawn, and you lazy asses are still in bed. Everyone up. Get dressed. We're going to eat something delicious. I made us reservations, and then we're going to have our surprise. Giovanna, you don't even need special clothes."

Maven leaned back on his elbows. "If you really wanted to be helpful, you could make coffee."

"Done. Downstairs. Get up. Move your body. It helps to wake you up. Take a shower." He walked out of the room.

Banyan smirked. "It's not his patients I worry about in the future, but his kids. Get up. Go to school," he mock yelled. "Actually, it would have been nice to have someone do that for me. My mother has never given a shit about my education."

Maven reached over me to shove him. "I care about your education. Chance cares. I bet Giovanna here cares. Your mom will only be happy if your father is supporting you for the rest of your life."

Banyan's phone dinged, and he rolled over to look at it. "Shit."

"What's wrong?" I touched his arm. "Bad news?"

"My mother is downstairs." He jumped out of bed, having paled considerably. "I've got to get down there before she rings the doorbell. If Chance answers, he'll never get away."

These guys really didn't like their mothers. Still shirtless and in his boxers, Banyan charged down the stairs at rapid speed. I could hear him pounding on the floors even when he was two staircases removed from us.

Maven shook his head. "If Chance thinks we're getting

out of here anytime soon, he has another think coming. The thing about Banyan's mom is that she is... how to say this delicately?"

I didn't need him to do that. "Just say it. She's what?"

"Dramatic." He got out of bed. "He saved me from mine. I'll help spare him some of his. Usually, when she's not with someone, she's in a rehab for some new ailment or in a detoxing place. Cleansing her soul or her body or her whatever. If they had punch cards for frequent visitors, she'd have one for every place in the world. It's all drama. It's all trying, still, to get Banyan's father to pay attention. He pays for anything she wants just to get her to leave him alone. All of it is done practically silently. No one should know about her or ask questions about the son he had out of wedlock."

I got out of bed. "Give me a few minutes, and I'll come down."

"Okay. You'll be a distraction to her but not necessarily a good one. She's not a woman who likes other pretty women. My mother can't stand her, and while I don't hold much by my mom's opinion, in this case, I think she's pretty right on."

The question I wanted to know was what I was going to have to go down to deal with. "How did she know he was here?"

Maven held up his phone. "My guess? We made the blogs last night. You in that dress. Banyan with you? She saw it this morning, and she knows if he's not at home, he's here. At least for now. Next year? That'll be different."

I thought of his loft. The guys didn't know about it yet, and that was his business to tell them. "Right. I'll still be in school. Trying to pass classes I hate to get back to my literature seminars."

He smirked. "Downstairs? She's a character that should be in one of your books."

———

MAVEN WASN'T WRONG. I suspected he almost never was. But I wouldn't put Ruby in my books. Not ever. She wasn't a character I wanted to spend any time with.

The brown-haired, brown-eyed stunner could probably stop New York City traffic with a blink of her eyes if she wanted to. She was tall, curvaceous, and appeared twenty years younger than she had to be, unless she'd had Banyan at ten years old.

She cried but not like I'd ever seen anyone cry before. When people wept, they did so with big, heart-wrenching sobs that took over their entire bodies. Or they were silent. Head in their hands, they shook without making a sound. Maybe they laughed through their tears. There were lots of ways that grief and sadness manifested themselves.

But Banyan's mother had her hand over her head on the couch while she leaned backward. Her face was passive except for tears that dropped down her face one little bit at a time. Her voice sounded distraught. She kept altering the volume of it.

I came down the stairs quietly, catching Chance's gaze when I did. He rolled his eyes at me then looked at Banyan's mom. The only person anywhere near her was her son. He sat on the other side of the couch.

Maven and Chance leaned on opposite walls. I stiffened my back. I'd gotten off easy with Maven's mom because Banyan had come and taken the heat off the whole thing. I could do this with Banyan's. We'd get this woman whatever it was she wanted and send her on her way. I wasn't always good at reading people correctly, but in this case, I was sure I was right.

Banyan's mom was here to make a scene. She was faking this outburst. That woman wasn't really upset.

"Hello." I kept my voice low. I wasn't dressed particularly nicely. I didn't have shoes or socks on, which made my feet cold, and I was in jeans and a plain, long sleeve, black t-shirt. My hair was pulled back. I didn't think other women ever found me threatening, but I'd gone out of my way to look really innocuous after Maven's statement about Banyan's mom.

Banyan jumped to his feet. "Mom, this is Giovanna. Giovanna, this is my mother, Haddi Lowen."

His mother stared at me without speaking, which left me to find my manners and handle this nonsense. I put out my hand. "It's so nice to meet Banyan's mom. I mean, I can hardly believe you're his mom. You don't look old enough to have children at all."

Banyan put his hand on the small of my back. Warmth spread up my spine. He was still in his boxer shorts, and I shot him a look. "Honey, do you want to go get dressed?"

He smirked at me. "Sure, sweetheart, I was just thinking maybe it was time to put on clothes. Do you want socks while I'm up there?"

I smiled my biggest fake grin. "Thanks."

"Welcome." Banyan tilted his head to the side and spoke to Chance and Maven. "You two will look after my girl, right?"

Chance cleared his throat. "For the two minutes you're upstairs? Sure. I think Mave and I can manage to see to it that Giovanna is okay. Hurry up."

Banyan's mother finally spoke as he rushed from the

room. "Well, Giovanna, you can't imagine as a mother how upsetting it is to see that your son is in town with his new..." She was trying to decide how to insult me. I could see the thought crossing right over her eyes. This woman was an open book. No, I decided right there. It took milliseconds. I wasn't going to let her. Once she said the word—skank, ho, slut— whatever it was, she couldn't take that back. We couldn't make this end productively. I was going to save her the angst.

I hugged her, hard. "Oh, I am so sorry, Ms. Lowen. How terribly distressing." She had a different last name than her son. She must have gotten married at some point to someone after she had Banyan to someone named Lowen. "Please forgive us. We whirled into town. And I'm sure Banyan was going to get in touch with you. He's so considerate that way."

I knew it was crazy. I had no business hugging this woman but sometimes the only way to deal with crazy was to simply be even crazier than the person doing the initial crazy stuff. I was thinking crazy a lot. That was fine. There were times that warranted it.

Banyan's mother stayed stiff for a second before she hugged me a little bit. We stepped apart. I sighed dramatically. "There's nothing to it. We're going to have to make this up to you. We'll come over bright and early tomorrow. We can have breakfast. Does six work? I really like to get up early."

Her hand went to her throat. "Breakfast?" She practically choked on the word. Women like Haddi never actually ate breakfast. My mother had told me that once, and up until this second, I hadn't known exactly what type of woman she referred to. In general, I didn't like to lump people into categories, but this woman had come over here to have a snit for no other reason than to have one. I could have bad thoughts about her if I wanted to.

She stepped back just as Banyan came down the stairs. "I'm going to pass on breakfast. But it was nice seeing you, and Banyan, maybe this year I will make it to visit you. Still haven't seen that place you call home during the school year."

His mother had never been there? Even mine had seen it five times. I didn't turn to look at him. If my parent had just made a statement like that, I'd prefer if all eyes weren't on me. But Banyan seemingly didn't flinch. Instead, he took his mother by the arm and escorted her from the house. A gush of wind flew inside, reminding me that it was really cold outside. A second later, Maven picked me up in his arms.

"I cannot believe you did that. I wasn't even sure for a few seconds what you were doing, but wow, you took the attitude right out of her. She had no idea what to do."

Maven set me down, and Chance pulled me against his side. "Pretty cool stuff there, Vonni. You should have seen her face. Breakfast? Hugs? She's going to be on the phone with her therapist in the Uber."

I shrugged. "I was just trying to diffuse the whole thing before everything exploded."

"Well, you did that." Banyan shut the door behind him as he walked into the house. "She's absolutely stunned. Told me you were quite different from what she expected."

He handed me my socks, which I gladly took. The floors were really cold. Almost like thinking about the temperature made the radiators turn on, the banging of the air coming out of the heating suddenly filled the room with obnoxious noise.

I sat down on the couch to put on my white cotton

socks, and Chance suddenly banged on the wall. "Okay, guys, seriously, we can't be late to this thing I planned. This is why I stick to pledges and don't do social events. Let's go. You all look great. Let's just get out of here."

Maven grinned at Banyan who swung his arm around Chance. It was Banyan who laughed when he spoke. "Look, it's stressed out type A Chance showing up here tonight. Sorry, bro, my mother has terrible timing. I thought for a minute she was going to have to come along except for the brilliant thinking of our girl here. Yes, where are we off to?"

Chance pointed to the door. "Grab your coats."

He was really being silent about this. I stood. "Can't wait."

I hadn't had a bad night with these guys, even when all it involved was watching sports I didn't quite understand and sipping small amounts of alcohol. I was really glad they'd decided I should be their friend. Even if I might never understand why.

Chance's planned night out started with incredible Chinese food. The restaurant was small inside and famous for pork. We ate ribs and laughed. I drank an entire beer, and it went to my head right away, which only made me want to eat more. Okay, I'd have to be careful with the stuff. But I laughed, listening to them all talk.

If any of them noticed that I tended not to talk at dinners out, they didn't comment. Maybe there would never really be a time that changed. One on one, I was fine. But something about the restaurant experience with more than one other person threw me off. I'd not ever stopped to think about why before.

In any case, it was nice to not worry they were going to try to draw me out. They didn't ignore me. In fact, Banyan had his arm around me the whole time and Maven kept knocking our shoes together under the table. Every once in a while, Chance would wink at me. This was easy. This was friendship.

I loved it.

Maybe ours was unconventional, but it was ours.

I swallowed. Was it all about to go away when we went back to school?

I forced the thought away. That was next week. This was now.

Maven's cell phone pinged as we were finishing up. "They've arrested someone for the fires. A homeless man who hung out near campus. They say it was him."

A homeless man? "How would he even get into the dorms or the frat? The security cards only let people in who have them or who are let in. Why was he starting fires?"

Maven shook his head. "I'll let you know when I get more information. Those are good questions."

I sighed. Something about that didn't sit well in my gut. Not that I was some kind of expert on solving mysteries, but I thought a whole lot about plot all the time. That seemed strange. But maybe life was weirder than fiction sometimes.

We ended up leaving the restaurant to go to Chelsea Piers for a while. I'd never been there. Rock climbing and bowling were things I loved to do, and I was thrilled. I had to bowl with my other arm because of the dislocated shoulder, and I had to watch the rock climbing, but it was so magical to be there. It was noisy, but the entire area had been dressed up in purples and golds for New Year's Eve.

By eleven at night, happiness had invaded my every pore. I didn't get the impression they did these things very much. Maven really couldn't bowl, although I'd never point that out, and Chance avoided the rock wall entirely. Banyan threw himself into activities with such fervor I couldn't tell if he was good at what he was doing and just being silly about it or not good and overcompensating. Either way, I knew I'd never forget the evening.

At eleven, Chance took my hand. We were apparently not done.

"There's more?" I couldn't believe it. This was plenty. Why add anything else to it.

Banyan looked at his watch. "We have to be somewhere for midnight? We're cutting it close for traffic, and seriously, Chance, we better not be going to Times Square. I'm not going to get into that mess. I'd rather watch it from home."

"Oh, we're going to watch it but not from home, and no, we're not exactly going to Times Square."

What did that mean? Banyan looked at Chance and put his hands on his hips. "You didn't."

Didn't what? I almost asked, and then Maven laughed. "You got the permits. Found someone to do it. The whole shebang. Just like you've been saying you were going to do for the last four years."

Chance grinned. "I've been saying it longer than four years. I just got serious about getting it done four years ago. Threw real money at the problem this year because I wanted to do it while we had Vonni with us."

"Guys," I finally got the words out. "What are we doing?"

Chance's smile, broadened. "We're going up in a helicopter. We're going to see New Year's Eve from the sky tonight."

I took a deep breath. "Wow."

Banyan put his hand on my back. "You've avoided my plane thus far. We never asked. Are you fearful of flying? Or heights?"

I shook my head. "No, actually. I used to do it all the

time. Going in a helicopter was never on my personal adventure list, but let's do it. Yes, sounds great. Why not? We only live once. And thank you, Chance. This is amazing! Thanks for organizing it. Thanks for the surprise."

His smile fell slightly, which I couldn't understand since I wanted to do what he planned. But when he spoke his words, he wasn't quite grinning anymore. "You're welcome, Vonni. This was my pleasure."

I'd never wanted to go in a helicopter. I knew my father wasn't a big fan of them. He used to have to take one back and forth to an island he was researching in Southeast Asia before he met my mother. If I hadn't been wearing headphones over my ears, it would have been uncomfortably loud. But New York was below us, and even though I'd never been much of a believer in anything, seeing the city lit up around and below us felt something akin to a religious experience. I couldn't really explain it. But there were millions of people down below us, living their lives, and for just a little while, I could see them from up above.

It was different on a plane. There were all kinds of restrictions on where the helicopter could go. Not directly over Times Square. Not directly over the East River. That was fine. I wasn't missing anything. In fact, I wasn't sure I'd ever look at this place the same way again.

I lifted my head to see if the guys were enjoying themselves, but all three of them stared at me. What were they thinking? I'd never be able to hear the over the sounds of the blades since my headphones didn't seem to be working, so I didn't ask.

A sudden sadness crept over me, and I did my best to hide the feeling from my expression. The vacation from myself was almost over. The truth was, we were all almost going back to school. I'd never spoken a word to any of them before that day on the street. Would that be different now? Would they still like me when I couldn't be this open?

I turned my attention back to the view. Life was simple above New York City.

JANUARY 7ᵗʰ
Maven

I ALMOST TURNED the car around and drove back to Manhattan. I'd delayed our return to school that morning so much that we'd hit rush hour traffic in New Jersey. I didn't even mind. That gave me more time with Giovanna. Sometimes, like today in the car, she was quiet. I always wanted to know what she was thinking, but being prodded to explain her private thoughts had to get old. She'd tell me if she wanted me to know.

I still couldn't really believe what had happened the last weeks. What had prompted me to run out onto the street and call out to her with that stupid name? That really wasn't like me. That was more a Banyan move, but I'd had no idea what to say, and I didn't want her to get away. It had felt like if I didn't stop her right that second, I'd never see her again.

Now here we were. In this strange relationship I'd never anticipated. The guys and I, we shared women. Maybe for a night. This ongoing sort of dating, sort of not dating thing? This was new. I didn't think she knew that, and I preferred it that way. Let her think we had this all together. She didn't need to know how much I worried that I'd lose her, that this couldn't be sustained as is for much longer.

How could this work, really, in the long run? She was going to have to pick one of us to date, or not date any of us and we'd all just become good friends. I hated everything about that.

Since I couldn't, unfortunately, control the universe, I had to concentrate on getting us through now. I wouldn't compete with Chance or Banyan. First off, they were my brothers. We'd lost a close friend together, and that had bonded us in a way others didn't really get. I knew them like I knew myself. I'd never hurt them. Deep inside of me, I wasn't exactly sure I would win if I did ask her to choose. Banyan and Chance were great guys. They were different than I was and would probably be better boyfriends.

She turned to look at me, raising her eyebrows in the way she did when she observed me, like she wanted to make me out somehow.

"You're upset."

I gave her a half smirk. "Who wants to go back to tests and finals? Papers? We have to get the pledges through this last bit to make them brothers. All of it is just... a lot."

She bit down on her lower lip. "I see."

Did she? "You'll come tonight, right? To the SPiI party? We have the best back to school one every January. Way better than the other houses." Did I even care about that anymore? Well, I did and I didn't. They'd elected me to care until May, so I was going to pull this shit off one way or another. "You can bring your friends. Text Banyan. We'll get them all on the list. No one with you waits in line."

I was rambling. *Damn it.*

"You want me to come?"

I loved the sound of her voice. "Are you kidding? Of course?"

You're my girl, library. Please don't disappear from my

life back to that place where I can't touch you, where I just see you from a distance. Please don't let me disappear back to whoever I was before I met you.

"Then I'll be there."

I let out a long breath. "Great. Cool. You'll have a good time."

We pulled up to her dorm. "Just like I promised. I got you back here."

She nodded. Her eyes were distant. It was hard for me to read her like this. "Thank you, Maven."

Anything, Giovanna. I'd do anything for you.

"Sure. See you tonight. If you want a ride, let me know. I'll send a pledge to get you." *Just say goodbye Maven, before she decides you're pathetic.* "See you later, library."

Her smile was huge. "See you later, SPiI."

She got out of the car, grabbed her bag, and walked into her dorm without turning around. She took my heart with her. My phone dinged. It was Banyan. He and Chance were back. We didn't have enough beer for the party, and three brothers needed to speak to me. I had to pull my shit together. And fast.

DO NOT FRET, dear reader. Part 2 of 3 is coming soon. What happens now that they're back at school? You'll have to wait to see. Sign up for my newsletter at www.rebeccaroyce.com and be on the lookout for Unexpected coming soon. Flip the page to see the list of all of my books!

OTHER BOOKS BY REBECCA ROYCE...

Wings of Artemis

Kidnapped By Her Husbands

Rescued by Their Wife

Crashing Into Destiny

Meeting Them

Reclaiming Their Love

Loving Them

Ship Called Malice

Saving Them

Dark Demise

Light Unfolding (coming soon)

Last Hope

Tradition Be Damned

Past Be Damned

Destiny Be Damned

Compassion Be Damned (coming soon)

Dragon Wars

Forever

Eternal

Always

Evermore

Endless

Wards and Wands

Hexed and Vexed

Curse Reversed (coming soon)

Safe Haven

Everywhere and Nowhere

More coming soon....

Soul Bound

Prisoner of the Dragons

More coming soon....

Shadow Promised

Strange Days

Weird Nights

Bizarre Years

More coming soon...

The Warrior

Initiation

Driven

Subversive

Redemption

Justice

Warrior World (spin off of The Warrior)

Deacon

Micah (coming soon)

The Westervelt Wolves

Her Wolf

Summer's Wolf

Wolf Reborn

Wolf's Valentine

Wolf's Magic

Alpha Wolf

Angel's Wolf

Darkest Wolf

Lone Wolf

Fallen Alpha

Alpha Rising

Alpha's Strength

Alpha's Sacrifice

Alpha's Truth

Alpha Enticing

Hidden Alpha (coming soon)

The Capes

Seductive Powers

Adrenaline Rush

Last Ascension

The Conditioned

Eye Contact

Embraced

Unlawful (coming soon...)

Cascade

Haunted Redemption

Phoenix Everlasting

Fragility Unearthed

Persuasion Enraptured

Reverse Harem Love Story

Unconventional (coming soon)

Unexpected (coming soon)

Stand Alone Titles

Planet Bear (coming soon)

Under The Lights

No Quitting Allowed

Mr. Wrong

Bite Marks

Bitten Surrender

The Vampire and The Virgin

Demon Within

Crimson Lust

Find Me (coming soon)